Praise for
Ian McEwan and *Black Dogs*

"Written with steely precision, taut and tense."
—*New York*

. . .

"[McEwan is] a master of menace, an excavator of the jagged fissures that lie just under civilization's crust."
—*Los Angeles Times Book Review*

. . .

"[McEwan's] cinematic images possess the gathering momentum of the montage in a Hitchcock thriller, and McEwan handles them with virtuosic brilliance."
—*The Boston Globe*

. . .

"Ian McEwan has long written with easy mastery about the dark side of things."
—*The Wall Street Journal*

. . .

"Subtle and unforgettable."
—*Voice Literary Supplement*

. . .

"A readable and lovely form of fictional rumination about moral and intellectual issues—smart, convincing and true."
—*Mirabella*

More Praise for *Black Dogs*

"Swift and flinty."
—*Time*

.   .   .

"McEwan is one of the decade's best fiction writers
. . . convincing and harrowing."
—*The Miami Herald*

.   .   .

"Provocative . . . impressive . . . haunting."
—*Publishers Weekly* (starred review)

.   .   .

"A novel of ideas with the hard edge of a thriller;
highly recommended."
—*Library Journal* (starred review)

.   .   .

"Subtly engaging . . . *Black Dogs* succeeds brilliantly."
—*New York Newsday*

Praise for *The Innocent*

"So exhaustively suspenseful . . . it should be devoured at one sitting."
—*Newsweek*

. . .

"McEwan . . . a breathtaking master . . . has written a blueprint for the future of the genre."
—*Time*

. . .

"Brilliant . . . will make the unsqueamish reader quiver with delighted dread."
—*Chicago Sun-Times*

. . .

"The sort of book Hitchcock might have snapped up for production."
—*USA Today*

. . .

"Wholly entertaining . . . brought together with the suspense and precision of a strong Hitchcock film, or a novel by Graham Greene."
—*The Wall Street Journal*

BANTAM BOOKS
NEW YORK   TORONTO   LONDON
SYDNEY   AUCKLAND

Ian McEwan

Black

Dogs

BLACK DOGS

A Bantam Book / published by arrangement with Doubleday

PUBLISHING HISTORY

Doubleday hardcover edition published November 1992
Bantam trade paperback edition / February 1994

Book design by Maria Carella

Library of Congress Cataloging-in-Publication Data

McEwan, Ian.
Black dogs / Ian McEwan.
p.   cm.
ISBN 0-553-37367-6 : $7.95
I. Title.
[PR6063.C4B5   1994]
823'.914—dc20   93-20992
CIP

Published simultaneously in the United States and Canada

PRINTED IN THE UNITED STATES OF AMERICA

OPM   0 9 8 7 6 5 4 3 2 1

To Jon Cook,
who saw them too.

.　　.　　.

In these times I don't, in a manner of
speaking, know what I want; perhaps I don't
want what I know and want what I don't know.

—*Marsilio Ficino,* letter to
Giovanni Cavalcanti, c. 1475

Preface

Ever since I lost mine in a road accident when I was eight, I have had my eye on other people's parents. This was particularly true during my teens, when many of my friends were casting off their own folk, and I did rather well in a lonely, hand-me-down way. In our neighborhood there was no shortage of faintly dejected fathers and mothers only too happy to have at least one seventeen-year-old around to appreciate their jokes, advice, cooking, even their money. At the same time I was something of a parent myself. My immediate milieu in those days was the new and disintegrating marriage of my sister, Jean, to a man called Harper. My protégée and intimate in this unhappy household was my three-year-old niece, Sally, Jean's only child. The rages and reconciliations that surged up and down the big apartment—Jean had inherited half the estate; my half was held in trust—tended to sweep Sally aside. Naturally, I identified with an abandoned child, and so we holed up nicely from time to time in a large room overlooking the garden, with her toys and my records, and a tiny kitchen we used whenever the savagery beyond made us not want to show our faces.

Looking after her was good for me. It kept me civilized and away from my own problems. Another two decades were to pass before I felt as rooted as I did then. Most of all I enjoyed the evenings when Jean and Harper were out, particularly in the summer, when I would read to Sally until she fell asleep, and later do my homework on the big table by the open French windows, facing out to the sweet smell of scented stock and traffic dust. I was studying for A levels at the Beamish on Elgin Crescent, a crammer's that liked to call itself an academy. When I looked up from my work and saw Sally behind me in the darkening room, on her back, sheets and teddies pushed down below her knees, arms and legs flung wide in what I took to be an attitude of completely misguided trust in the benevolence of her world, I was elated by a wild and painful protectiveness, a stab in the heart, and I am sure it was for this that I have had four children of my own. I never had any doubts about it: at some level you remain an orphan for life; looking after children is one way of looking after yourself.

Unpredictably, Jean would burst in on us, powered by guilt or by a surplus of love from making peace with Harper, and she would bear Sally away to their end of the apartment with coos and hugs and worthless promises. That was when the blackness, the hollow feeling of unbelonging, was likely to come down. Rather than skulk about or watch TV like other kids, I would slope off into the night, down Ladbroke Grove, to the household currently warmest to me. The images that come to mind after more than twenty-five years are of pale stuccoed mansions, some peeling, others immaculate, Powis Square perhaps, and a rich yellow light from the open front door revealing in the darkness a white-faced adolescent, already six feet tall, shuffling inside his Chelsea boots. Oh, good evening, Mrs. Langley. Sorry to trouble you. Is Toby in?

More likely than not Toby is with one of his girls, or in the pub with friends, and I am backing off down the porch steps with my apologies until Mrs. Langley calls me back with 'Jeremy, would you like to come in anyway? Come on, have a drink with boring old us. I know Tom will be pleased to see you.'

Ritual demurrals, and the six-foot cuckoo is in, and being led across the hall to a huge, book-crammed room with Syrian daggers, a shaman's mask, an Amazonian blowpipe with curare-tipped darts. Here Toby's forty-three-year-old father sits under a lamp reading untranslated Proust or Thucydides or Heine by an open window. He is smiling as he stands and extends his hand.

'Jeremy! How nice to see you. Have a scotch and water with me. Sit down over there and listen to this, tell me what you think.'

And eager to engage me in talk that bears on my subjects (French, history, English, Latin), he turns back a few pages to some awesome convolution from *A L'ombre des jeunes filles en fleurs,* and I, equally eager to show off and be accepted, rise to the challenge. Good-humoredly, he corrects me, then later we might consult Scott-Moncrieff and Mrs. Langley will come in with sandwiches and tea and they will ask after Sally and want to know the latest between Harper and Jean, whom they have never met.

Tom Langley was a diplomat with the Foreign Office, posted home to Whitehall after three tours of duty abroad. Brenda Langley ran their beautiful home and gave lessons in the harpsichord and piano. Like many of the parents of my friends from the Beamish Academy, they were educated and well-off. What an exquisite, desirable combination that seemed to me, whose background was middling income and no books.

But Toby Langley did not appreciate his parents at all. He was bored by their civilized, intellectually curious, open-minded ways, and by his spacious, orderly home, and by his interesting childhood spent in the Middle East, Kenya, and Venezuela. He was halfheartedly studying two A levels (maths and art) and said he did not want to go to university at all. He cultivated friends from the new high-rises toward Shepherd's Bush, and his girlfriends were waitresses, and shop assistants with sticky beehive hairdos. He pursued chaos and trouble by going out with several girls at once. He worked up a dim-witted mode of speech complete with glottal *t*'s and 'I fink' and 'I goes to him' for 'I said to him,' which became an ingrained habit. Since he was my friend I said nothing, but he caught my disapproval.

Though I maintained the pretext of calling on Toby when he was out, and Mrs. Langley colluded with such protocols as 'You might as well come in,' I was always welcome at

Powis Square. Sometimes I was asked to give an insider's opinion on Toby's waywardness, and I would sound off disloyally and priggishly about Toby's need to 'find himself.' Similarly, I inhabited the home of the Silversmiths, neo-Freudian psychoanalysts, man and wife, with amazing ideas about sex, and an American-sized fridge jam-packed with delicacies, whose three teenage children, two girls and a boy, were crazy louts who ran a shoplifting and playground extortion racket up at Kensal Rise. I was comfortable too in the big untidy home of my friend Joseph Nugent, also of the Beamish Academy. His father was an oceanographer who led expeditions to the uncharted seabeds of the world, his mother the first woman columnist on the *Daily Telegraph,* but Joe thought his parents were dull beyond belief and preferred a gang of lads from Notting Hill who were happiest of an evening polishing up the multiple headlamps on their Lambretta scooters.

Were all these parents attractive to me simply because they were not mine? Try as I might, I could not answer yes, for they were undeniably likeable. They interested me, I picked things up. At the Langleys' I learned of sacrificial practices in the Arabian desert, improved my Latin and French, and first heard the Goldberg Variations. At the Silversmiths' I heard tell of the polymorphous perverse, and was enraptured by tales of Dora, Little Hans, and the Wolf man, and ate lox, bagels and cream cheese, latkes, and borscht. At the Nugents', Janet talked me through the Profumo scandal and persuaded me to learn shorthand; her husband once gave an imitation of a man suffering the bends. These people treated me like a grown-up. They poured me drinks, offered me their cigarettes, asked my opinions. They were all in their forties, tolerant, relaxed, energetic. It was Cy Silversmith who taught me to play tennis. If any pair of them had been my parents (if only), I was certain I would have liked them more.

And if my parents had been alive, would I not have been breaking for freedom like the rest? Again, I could not answer yes. What my friends were pursuing seemed to me the very antithesis of freedom, a masochistic lunge at downward social mobility. And how irritatingly predictable of my contemporaries, especially of Toby and Joe, that they should consider my domestic setup a very paradise: the stinking coven of our uncleaned apartment, its licentious late-morning gin, my stunning, chain-smoking sister, a Jean Harlow look-alike, one of the first of her generation into a miniskirt, the adult drama of her hammer-blow, whip-crack marriage, and sadistic Harper, the leather feticheur with red-and-black tattoos of strutting cockerels on his tuberous forearms, and no one there to nag about the state of my room, my clothes, my diet, or my whereabouts, or my schoolwork or my prospects or my mental or dental health. What more could I want? Nothing, except, they might add, to be shot of that kid who was always hanging around.

Such was the symmetry of our respective disaffections that it happened one winter's evening that Toby was at my place, pretending to relax in the freezing squalor of our kitchen, smoking cigarettes and attempting to impress Jean— who, it should be said, detested him, with his voice of the people—while I was at his, comfortable on the chesterfield in front of an open fire, a glass of his father's single malt warming in my hand, under my shoeless feet the lovely Bokhara that Toby claimed was a symbol of cultural rape, listening to Tom Langley's account of a deadly poisonous spider and the death throes of a certain third secretary on the first landing of the British embassy in Caracas, while across the hall, through open doors, we heard Brenda at one of Scott Joplin's lilting, syncopated rags, which at that time were being redis-covered and had not yet been played to death.

I realize that much of the above tells against me, that it is Toby pursuing in impossible circumstances a beautiful crazy young woman beyond his reach, or his and Joe's and the Silversmith kids' excursions into the neighborhood, that dis-play a proper appetite for life, and that a seventeen-year-old's infatuation with comfort and the conversation of his elders suggests a dull spirit; and that in describing this period of my life I have unconsciously mimicked not only, here and there, the superior, sneering attitudes of my adolescent self, but also the rather formal, distancing, labyrinthine tone in which I used to speak, clumsily derived from my scant reading of Proust, which was supposed to announce me to the world as an intellectual. All I can say for my younger self is that al-though I was hardly aware of it at the time, I missed my par-ents terribly. I had to build up my defenses. Pomposity was one of them; another was my cultivated disdain for my friends' activities. They could range freely because they were secure; I needed the hearths they had deserted.

I was prepared to do without girls, partly because I thought they would distract me from my work. I rightly as-sumed that the surest route out of my situation—by which I mean living with Jean and Harper—was university, and for that I needed A levels. I worked fanatically, putting in two, three, even four hours a night long before the run-up to exams. Another reason for my timidity was that my sister's first moves in that direction, when I was eleven and she was fifteen and we were living with our aunt, had been so noisily successful, with a faceless horde processing through the bedroom we were supposed to share (our aunt finally ejected us both), that I felt quite cowed. In that apportioning of experience and expertise that goes on between siblings, Jean had spread her beautiful limbs—to adapt Kafka's formulation—across my map of the world and obliterated the territory marked 'sex,' so that I was obliged to voyage elsewhere—to obscure islets marked Catullus, Proust, Powis Square.

And I did have my affair of the heart with Sally. With her I felt responsible and intact, and I did not need anyone else. She was a pale little girl. No one took her out much; when I came in from school I never felt like it, and Jean was not at all keen on outdoors. Much of the time I played with Sally in our big room. She had the three-year-old girl's imperious manner. 'Not on the chair! Come down here on the floor with me.' We played Hospitals, or Houses, or Lost in the Woods, or Sailing to a New Place. Sally kept up a breathless narrative of our whereabouts, our motives, our sudden metamorphoses. 'You're not a monster, you're a king.' Then we might hear from the far end of the apartment a shout of rage from Harper, followed by a yelp of pain from Jean, and Sally would render a perfect, miniature adult grimace, a beautifully timed wince-*cum*-shrug, and say in the melodiously pure tones of a voice still new to grammatical construction, 'Mummy and Daddy! What silly billies they are being again!'

And indeed they were. Harper was a security guard who claimed to be studying for an external degree in anthropology. Jean had married him when she was barely twenty and Sally was eighteen months. The following year, when Jean's money came through, she bought the flat and lived off the change. Harper gave up his job, and the two of them hung around all day, drinking, fighting, making up. Harper had a gift for violence. There were times when I looked uneasily at my sister's red cheek or swollen lip and thought of obscure manly codes that required me to challenge my brother-in-law and defend her honor. But there were also times when I went into the kitchen and found Jean at the table reading a magazine and smoking while Harper stood at the kitchen sink, naked but for his purple jock strap, with half a dozen bright red weals across his buttocks, humbly washing the dishes. I was grateful to acknowledge that I was out of my depth, and I retreated to the big room and the games with Sally that I could understand.

I shall never understand why I did not know or guess that Jean and Harper's violence extended to my niece. That she let twenty years go by before she told anyone shows how suffering can isolate a child. I did not know then how adults can set about children, and perhaps I would not have wanted to know; I would be leaving soon, and already my guilt was growing. By the end of that summer, soon after my eighteenth birthday, Harper had left for good and I had my A levels and a place at Oxford. I should have been overjoyed a month later when I carried out my books and records from the apartment to a friend's van; my two-year plan had worked, I was out, I was free. But Sally's dogged, suspicious questions as she tracked me backward and forward between our room and the pavement were an indictment of betrayal. 'Where are you going? Why are you going? When are you coming back?' To this last, sensing my evasiveness, my clotted silence, she returned again and again. And when she thought to lure me back, to divert me from a history degree with the suggestion, so pertly, so optimistically put, that we play instead Sailing to a New Place, I put down my armful of books and ran out to the van to sit in the passenger seat and weep. I thought I knew only too well just how she felt, or how she would feel: it was nearly midday and Jean was still sleeping off the gin and pills with which she was mourning Harper's departure. I would wake her before I left, but in some important respect Sally was on her own. And so she remains.

Neither Sally, Jean, nor Harper play a part in what follows. Nor do the Langleys, Nugents, or Silversmiths. I left them all behind. My guilt, my sense of betrayal, would not permit me to return to Notting Hill, not even for a weekend. I could not bear to undergo another parting from Sally. The thought that I was inflicting on her the very loss I had suffered myself intensified my loneliness, and obliterated the excitement of my first term. I became a quietly depressed student, one of those dull types practically invisible to their contemporaries, apparently excluded by the very laws of nature from the process of making friends. I made for the nearest hearth. This one was in North Oxford and belonged to a fatherly tutor and his wife. For a short while I shone there, and a few people told me I was clever. But this was not enough to stop me leaving, North Oxford first, then, in my fourth term, the university itself. For years afterward I continued to leave—addresses, jobs, friends, lovers. Occasionally I managed to obscure my irreducible sense of childish unbelonging by making friends with someone's parents. I would be invited in, I would come to life, then I would leave.

This sorry madness came to an end with my marriage, in my mid thirties, to Jenny Tremaine. My existence began. Love, to borrow Sylvia Plath's phrase, set me going. I came to

life for good, or rather, life came to me; I should have
learned from my experience with Sally that the simplest way
of restoring a lost parent was to become one yourself, that to
succor the abandoned child within, there was no better way
than having children of your own to love. And just when I no
longer had need of them, I acquired parents in the form of
in-laws, June and Bernard Tremaine. But there was no
hearth. When I first met them they were living in separate
countries and were barely on speaking terms. June had long
before retreated to a remote hilltop in southern France and
was about to become very ill. Bernard was still a public figure
who did all his entertaining in restaurants. They rarely saw
their children. For their part, Jenny and her two brothers had
despaired of their parents.

The habits of a lifetime could not be instantly erased.
Somewhat to Jenny's annoyance, I persisted in a friendship
with June and Bernard. In conversations with them over several years, I discovered that the emotional void, the feeling of
belonging nowhere and to no one that had afflicted me between the ages of eight and thirty-seven, had had an important intellectual consequence: I had no attachments, I
believed in nothing. It was not that I was a doubter, or that I
had armed myself with the useful skepticism of a rational
curiosity, or that I saw all arguments from all sides; there was
simply no good cause, no enduring principle, no fundamental idea with which I could identify, no transcendent entity
whose existence I could truthfully, passionately, or quietly as-
sert.

Unlike June and Bernard. They began together as communists, then went their separate ways. But their capacity,
their appetite for belief never diminished. Bernard was a

gifted entomologist; all his life he remained committed to the elation and limited certainties of science; he replaced his communism with thirty years' devoted advocacy of numerous causes for social and political reform. June came to God in 1946 through an encounter with evil in the form of two dogs. (Bernard found this construction of the event almost too embarrassing to discuss.) A malign principle, a force in human affairs that periodically advances to dominate and destroy the lives of individuals or nations, then retreats to await the next occasion—it was a short step from this to a luminous countervailing spirit, benign and all-powerful, residing within and accessible to us all; perhaps not so much a step as a simultaneous recognition. Both principles were incompatible, she felt, with the materialism of her politics, and she left the party.

Whether June's black dogs should be regarded as a potent symbol, a handy catch phrase, evidence of her credulity, or a manifestation of a power that really exists, I cannot say. In this memoir I have included certain incidents from my own life—in Berlin, Majdanek, Les Salces, and St. Maurice de Navacelles—that are open equally to Bernard's and to June's kind of interpretation. Rationalist and mystic, commissar and yogi, joiner and abstainer, scientist and intuitionist, Bernard and June are the extremities, the twin poles along whose slippery axis my own unbelief slithers and never comes to rest. In Bernard's company, I always sensed there was an element missing from his account of the world, and that it was June who held the key. The assurance of his skepticism, his invincible atheism, made me wary; it was too arrogant, too much was closed off, too much denied. In conversations with June, I found myself thinking like Bernard; I felt stifled by her expressions of faith, and bothered by the unstated assumption of all believers that they are good because they believe what they believe, that faith is virtue and, by extension, unbelief is unworthy, or at best pitiable.

It will not do to argue that rational thought and spiritual insight are separate domains and that opposition between them is falsely conceived. Bernard and June often talked to me about ideas that could never sit side by side. Bernard, for example, was certain that there was no direction, no patterning in human affairs or fates other than that which was imposed by human minds. June could not accept this; life had a purpose and it was in our interests to open ourselves to it. Nor will it do to suggest that both these views are correct. To believe everything, to make no choices, amounts to much the same thing, to my mind, as believing in nothing at all.

I am uncertain whether our civilization at this turn of the millennium is cursed by too much or too little belief, whether people like Bernard and June cause the trouble, or people like me.

But I would be false to my own experience if I did not declare my belief in the possibility of love transforming and redeeming a life. I dedicate this memoir to my wife, Jenny, and to Sally, my niece, who continues to suffer the consequences of her childhood; may she too find this love.

I married into a divided family in which the children, in the interests of self-preservation, had to a degree turned their backs on their parents. My tendency to play the cuckoo caused some unhappiness to Jenny and her brothers, for which I apologize. I have taken a number of liberties, the most flagrant of which has been to recount certain conversations never intended for the record. But then, the occasions when I announced to others, or even to myself, that I was 'on the job' were so rare that a few indiscretions became an absolute necessity. It is my hope that June's ghost, and Bernard's too—if some essence of his consciousness, against all his convictions, persists—will forgive me.

1

· · · · · · · · · · · ·

Wiltshire

T he framed picture June Tremaine kept on the locker by her bed was there to remind herself, as much as inform her visitors, of the pretty girl whose face, unlike her husband's, gave no indication of the direction it was set to take. The snapshot dates from 1946, a day or two after their wedding and a week before they set off on their honeymoon to Italy and France. The couple are arm in arm by the railings near the entrance to the British Museum. Perhaps it was their lunch break, for they both worked nearby, and they were not given permission to leave their jobs until a few days before they set off. They lean in toward each other with a quaint concern for being cut off at the edges of the picture. Their smiles at the camera are of genuine delight. Bernard you could not possibly mistake. Then as always, six foot three, outsized hands and feet, a preposterous, good-natured jaw, and jug-handle ears made even more comical by the pseudomilitary haircut. Forty-three years did only predictable damage, and that only at the margins—thinner hair, thicker eyebrows, coarser skin—while the essential man, the astonishing apparition, was the same clumsy beaming giant in 1946 as in 1989, when he asked me to take him to Berlin.

June's face, however, veered from its appointed course much as her life did, and it is barely possible to discern in the snapshot the old face benignly wreathing into welcome when one entered her private room. The twenty-five-year-old woman has a sweet round face and a jolly smile. Her going-away perm is too tight, too prim, and does not suit her at all. Spring sunshine illuminates the strands that are already cutting loose. She wears a short jacket with high padded shoulders and a matching pleated skirt, the timid extravagance of cloth associated with the postwar New Look. Her white blouse has a wide open V neck daringly tapered to her cleavage. The collar is turned back outside the jacket to give her the breezy, English rose look of girls on wartime posters. From 1938 she was a member of the Socialist Cycling Club of Amersham. One arm tucks her handbag into her side, the other arm is linked with her man's. She leans against him, her head well short of his shoulder.

The photograph now hangs in the kitchen of our house in the Languedoc. I have often studied it, usually when alone. Jenny, my wife, June's daughter, suspects my predatory nature and is irritated by my fascination with her parents. She has spent long enough getting free of them and she is right to feel that my interest might be dragging her back. I put my face up close, trying to see the future life, the future face, the single-mindedness that followed a singular act of courage. The cheery smile has forced a tiny pucker of skin in the creaseless forehead, directly above the space between the eyebrows. In later life it was to become the dominant feature in a seamy face, a deep vertical fold that rose from the bridge of her nose to divide her forehead. Perhaps I am only imagining the hardness beneath the smile, buried in the line of the jaw, a firmness, a fixity of opinion, a scientific optimism about the future; the photograph was taken the morning June and Bernard signed up as members of the Communist party of Great Britain at the headquarters in Gratton Street. They are leaving their jobs and are free to declare their allegiances, which throughout the duration of the war have wavered. Now, when many have their doubts after the party's vacillations—was the war a noble liberating antifascist cause or predatory imperialist aggression?—and some are resigning their membership, June and Bernard have taken the plunge. Beyond all their hopes for a sane, just world free of war and class oppression, they feel that belonging to the party associates them with all that is youthful, lively, intelligent, and daring. They are heading off across the Channel to the chaos of Northern Europe, where they have been advised not to go. But they are determined to test their new liberties, personal and geographical. From Calais they will be making south for the Mediterranean spring. The world is new and at peace, fascism has been the irrefutable evidence of capitalism's terminal crisis, the benign revolution is at hand, and they are young, just married, and in love.

Bernard persisted with his membership, with much agonizing, until the Soviet invasion of Hungary in 1956. Then he considered his resignation long overdue. This change of heart represented a well-documented logic, a history of disillusion shared by a whole generation. But June lasted only a few months, until the confrontation on her honeymoon that gave this memoir its title, and hers was a profound alteration, a metempsychosis mapped in the transformation of her face. How did a round face become so long? Could it really have been the life, rather than the genes, that caused that little crease above the eyebrows pushed up by her smile to take root and produce the wrinkle tree that reached right to the hairline? Her own parents had nothing so strange in their old age. By the end of her life, by the time she was installed at the nursing home, it was a face to match the elderly Auden's. Perhaps years of Mediterranean sunshine toughened and buckled the complexion, and years of solitude and reflection distended the features, then folded them in on themselves. The nose lengthened with the face, and the chin did too, then seemed to change its mind and attempt the return by growing outward in a curve. In repose her face had a chiseled, sepulchral look; it was a statue, a mask carved by a shaman to keep at bay the evil spirit.

In this last there may have been some simple truth. She might have grown her face to accommodate her conviction that she had confronted and been tested by a symbolic form of evil. 'No, you clot. Not symbolic!' I hear her correcting me. 'Literal, anecdotal, true. Don't you know, I was nearly killed!'

·   ·   ·

I do not know if this was actually the case or not, but in memory each of my few visits to her in the nursing home in the spring and summer of 1987 took place on days of rain and high wind. Perhaps there was only one such day, and it has blown itself across the others. On each occasion, it seems, I entered the place—a mid-Victorian country house—at a run from the car park, set too far away by the stable block. The old horse chestnuts were roaring and shaking, the uncut grass was flattened, silver sides up, against the ground. I had pulled my jacket over my head, and I was damp and hot with irritation at another disappointing summer. I paused in the entrance hall, waiting to get my breath and for my temper to settle. Was it really just the rain? I would be pleased to see June, but the place itself brought me down. Its tiredness reached into my bones. The oak-effect paneling pressed in on all sides, and the carpet, patterned in kinetic swirls of red and musty yellow, rose up to assault my eye and restrict my breathing. The uncirculated air, held in long-term residence by a system of regulation firebreak doors, carried in suspension the accreted flavors of bodies, clothes, perfumes, fried breakfasts. A shortage of oxygen made me yawn; did I have the energy for the visit? I could as easily have passed the untended reception desk and wandered the corridors until I found an empty room and a bed made up. I would slip between the institutional sheets. Check-in formalities would be concluded later, after I had been woken for my supper, brought on a rubber-wheeled trolley. Afterward, I would take a sedative and doze again. The years would slip by . . .

At this, a minor flutter of panic restored me to my purpose. I crossed to the reception desk and struck the sprung bell with the flat of my palm. It was another false touch, this antique hotel bell. The intended atmosphere was that of a country retreat; the achieved effect was that of an overgrown bed-and-breakfast, the kind of place where the bar is a locked cupboard in the dining room, open at seven o'clock for one hour. And behind these divergent presentations was the reality itself—a profitable nursing home specializing, without the wholesome confidence to acknowledge the fact in its literature, in the care of the terminally ill.

A small-print complication in the policy and the insurance company's surprising severity deprived June of the hospice she had wanted. Everything about her return to England some years before had been complicated and distressing. There was the tortuous route we took to a final confirmation, with reversals of expert opinion along the way, that she had an untreatable disease, a relatively rare form of leukemia; Bernard's distress; transporting her possessions from France and separating from them the unwanted junk; finances, property, accommodation; a legal fight with the insurance company, which had to be abandoned; a series of difficulties in the sale of June's London flat; long car trips north for treatment from a dim elderly fellow said to have the power of healing in his hands. June insulted him and these same hands almost slapped her face. The first year of my marriage was completely overshadowed. Jenny and I, as well as her brothers and friends of Bernard and June's, were drawn into the vortex, a furious expense of nervous energy we mistook for efficiency. Only when Jenny gave birth to our first child, Alexander, in 1983, did we—Jenny and I, at least—come to our senses.

The receptionist appeared and gave me the visitor's

book to sign. Five years on, June was still alive. She could have lived in her Tottenham Court Road flat. She should have stayed in France. She was, so Bernard remarked, taking as much time over dying as the rest of us. But the flat had been sold, the arrangements were in place, and the space she had made around her in life had been closed off, filled in by our worthy efforts. She chose to remain in a nursing home where staff and death-bound residents alike consoled themselves with magazines and TV quiz shows and soaps booming off the glossy, pictureless, bookless walls of the recreation room. Our mad arranging had been nothing more than evasion. No one had wanted to contemplate the appalling fact. No one but June. After her return from France, and before the nursing home was found, she moved in with Bernard and worked on the book she was hoping to finish. No doubt she also practiced the meditations she described in her popular pamphlet, *Ten Meditations*. She had been content to let us spin about with the practicalities. When her strength ebbed far more slowly than medically predicted, she was equally content to accept the Chestnut Reach Nursing Home as uniquely her responsibility. She had no wish to move out, back into the world. She claimed that her life was usefully simplified, and that her isolation in a house of TV watchers suited her, even did her good. Moreover, it was her fate.

Despite what Bernard had said, now, in 1987, she was fading. She spent far more time this year asleep during the day. Although she pretended otherwise, the only writing she was doing was in her notebooks, and there was little of that. She no longer walked the neglected footpath through the woods to the nearest village. She was sixty-seven. At forty I had just reached the age myself when one begins to differentiate between the stages of later life. There had been a time when I would have regarded it as plainly untragic to be ill and dying in your late sixties, hardly worth struggling against or complaining about. You're old, you die. Now I was beginning to see that you hung on at every stage—forty, sixty, eighty—until you were beaten, and that sixty-seven can be early in the end game. June still had things to do. She had been looking well as an elderly woman in the south of France—that Easter Island face under a straw hat, the natural authority of unhurried movement as she made the early evening inspection of her gardens, the afternoon sleeps chiming with local practice.

As I trod the bilious, swirling carpet, which continued out of the hall, under the wire mesh glass fire door, along the corridor to cover every available inch of public space, it came to me again how deeply I resented the fact that she was dying. I was *against* it, I could not accept it. She was my adopted mother, the one that love for Jenny, marriage conventions, fate, had allotted me, my thirty-two-years-late replacement.

For over two years I had made my infrequent visits alone. Jenny and her mother found even twenty minutes of bedside chat a forced march. Slowly, far too slowly as it turned out, there emerged from my meandering conversations with June the possibility of a memoir I would write. The idea embarrassed the rest of the family. One of Jenny's brothers tried to dissuade me. I was suspected of wanting to threaten a difficult truce by turning up forgotten quarrels. The children could not conceive how so wearingly familiar a subject as their parents' differences could hold its fascination. They need not have worried. In the uncontrollable way of daily life, it worked out that there were only two visits toward the end when I managed to get June to talk about the past in an organized fashion, and from the very beginning we had quite different notions of what the true subject of my account should be.

In the bag of shopping I had brought her, along with the fresh litchis from Soho market, Montblanc black ink, the 1762–63 volume of Boswell's *Journal,* Brazilian coffee, and half a dozen bars of expensive chocolate, was my notebook. She would not permit a tape recorder. I suspected she wanted to feel free to be rude about Bernard, for whom she felt love and irritation in equal measure. He usually rang when he knew I had been to see her. 'Dear boy, what's the state of mind?' By which he meant that he wanted to know if she had been talking about him, and in what terms. For my part, I was glad to be without boxes of tapes in my study filled with compromising proof of June's occasional indiscretions. For example, long before the idea of a memoir had taken hold, she had shocked me once by announcing in a suddenly lowered voice, as a key to all his imperfections, that Bernard 'took a small penis size.' I was not inclined to interpret her literally. She had been angry with him that day, and besides, his, I was certain, was the only one she had ever seen. It was the phrasing that struck me, the suggestion that it had been mere obstinacy in her husband that had prevented him from ordering something more capacious from his regular suppliers in Jermyn Street. In a notebook the remark could be encoded in shorthand. On tape it would have been simple evidence of a betrayal, one that I would have needed to keep in a locked cupboard.

As though to emphasize her separation from what she called the 'other inmates,' her room was at the far end of the corridor. I slowed as I approached it. I could never quite believe that I was going to find her here, behind one of these identical plywood doors. She belonged where I first saw her, among the lavender and box of her property, on the edge of a wilderness. I tapped lightly on the door with a fingernail. She would not want me to think she had been dozing. She preferred to be discovered among her papers and books. I knocked a little harder. I heard a stirring, a murmur, a creak of bedsprings. A third knock. A pause, a throat clearing, another pause, then she called me to enter. She was just pulling herself upright in the bed as I went in. She gaped at me without recognition. Her hair was a mess. She had been buried in a sleep that had itself been smothered in an illness. I thought I should leave her to collect herself, but it was too late now. In the few seconds that it took to approach slowly and set down my bag, she had to reconstruct her whole existence, who and where she was, how and why she came to be in this small white-walled room. Only when she had all that could she begin to remember me. Beyond her window, anxious to prompt her, a horse chestnut was waving its limbs. Perhaps it succeeded only in confusing her further, for today she was taking longer than usual to come to. A few books and several sheets of blank paper lay across the bed. She ordered them feebly, playing for time.

'June, it's Jeremy. I'm sorry, I got here earlier than I thought.'

Suddenly, she had it all at once, but she concealed it with a bout of unconvincing cantankerousness. 'Yes, you bloody well are. I was trying to remember what it was I was about to write.' She put no effort into the performance. We were both aware she had no pen in her hand.

'Would you like me to come back in ten minutes?'

'Don't be ridiculous. I've lost it now for good. It was rubbish anyway. Sit down. What have you got me? Did you remember my ink?' As I pulled up my chair, she allowed herself the smile she had been holding back. The face creased into the complexity of a fingerprint as her lips pushed across her cheeks whorls of parallel lines that encircled her features and curled round to her temples. In the center of her forehead the main trunk of the wrinkle tree deepened to a furrow.

I set out my purchases and she examined each with a jokey remark or little question that needed no answer.

'Now why should the Swiss of all people be good at making chocolate? Just what is it that's been giving me this craving for litchis? Do you think I could be pregnant?'

These tokens from the outside world did not sadden her. Her exclusion from it was complete and, as far as I could tell, without regret. It was a country she had left forever and in which she retained no more than a fond and lively interest. I did not know how she could bear it, giving up so much, settling for the dullness here: the ruthlessly boiled vegetables, the fussy, clucking old folk, the dazed gluttony of their TV watching. After a life of such self-sufficiency, I would be panicking, or constantly planning my escape. However, her acquiescence, which was almost serene, made her easy company. There was no guilt at leaving, or even at postponing a visit. She had transplanted her independence to the confines of her bed, where she read, wrote, meditated, dozed. She required only to be taken seriously.

At Chestnut Reach this was not as simple as it sounds, and it took her months to persuade the nurses and helpers. It was a struggle I thought she was bound to lose; condescension is all to the professional carer's power. June succeeded because she never lost her temper and became the child they intended her to be. She was calm. When a nurse walked into her room without knocking—I saw this once—singsonging in the first person plural, June held the young woman's gaze and radiated a forgiving silence. In the early days she was marked down as a difficult patient. There was even talk of Chestnut Reach's being unable to continue with her. Jenny and her brothers came to confer with the director. June refused a part in the conversation. She had no intention of moving. Her certainty was authoritative, tranquil, born of years of thinking things through alone. She converted her doctor first. Once he realized that this was not one more witless old biddy, he began talking to her of nonmedical matters—wildflowers, for which they both had a passion and on which she was an expert. Soon he was confiding marital problems. The staff's attitude to June was transformed. Such is the hierarchical nature of medical establishments.

I regarded it as a triumph of tactics, of thinking ahead; by concealing her irritation she had won through. But it was not a tactic, she told me when I congratulated her, it was an attitude of mind she had learned long ago from Lao-tzu's *The Way of Tao*. It was a book she recommended from time to time, though whenever I looked at it, it never failed to irritate me with its smug paradoxes: to attain your goal, walk in the opposite direction. On this occasion she took up her book and read aloud, ' "The Way of heaven excels in overcoming though it does not contend." '

I said, 'Just what I'd expect.'

'Shut up. Listen to this. "Of two sides raising arms against each other, it is the one that is sorrow-stricken that wins." '

'June, the more you say, the less I understand.'

'Not bad. I'll make a sage of you yet.'

When she was satisfied that I had brought exactly what she had ordered, I stowed the goods, except for the ink, which she kept on the locker. The heavy fountain pen, the grayish white cartridge paper, and the black ink were the only visible reminders of her former daily life. Everything else— her delicatessen luxuries, her clothes—had its special place, out of sight. Her study at the *bergerie,* with its views westward down the valley toward St. Privat, was five times the size of this room and could barely accommodate her books and papers; beyond, the huge kitchen with its *jambons de montagne* hanging from beams, demijohns of olive oil on the stone floor, and scorpions sometimes nesting in the cupboards; the living room, which took up all of the old barn where a hundred locals had once gathered at the end of a boar hunt; her bedroom with the four-poster bed and French windows of stained glass, and the guest bedrooms, through all of which, over the years, her possessions flowed and spread; the room where she pressed her flowers; the hut with gardening tools in the orchard of almonds and olives, and near that, the henhouse that looked like a miniature dovecote—all this boiled down, stripped away, to one freestanding bookcase, a tallboy of clothes she never wore, a steamer trunk no one was allowed to look inside, and a tiny fridge.

While I unwrapped the fruit and washed it at the handbasin and put it with the chocolate in the fridge and found a place, *the* place, for the coffee, I conveyed messages from Jenny, love from the children. She asked after Bernard, but I had not seen him since my last visit. She arranged her hair with her fingers and settled the pillows around her. When I returned to the chair by her bed I found myself looking once more at the framed photograph on the locker. I too could have fallen in love with that round-faced beauty with the overtrained hair, the delighted, jaunty smile grazing the biceps of her loved one. It was the innocence that was so appealing, not only of the girl, or the couple, but of the time itself; even the blurred shoulder and head of a suited passerby had a naive, unknowing quality, as did a frog-eyed saloon car parked in a street of premodern emptiness. The innocent time! Tens of millions dead, Europe in ruins, the extermination camps still a news story, not yet our universal reference point of human depravity. It is photography itself that creates the illusion of innocence. Its ironies of frozen narrative lend to its subjects an apparent unawareness that they will change or die. It is the future they are innocent of. Fifty years on we look at them with the godly knowledge of how they turned out after all—who they married, the date of their death—with no thought for who will one day be holding photographs of us.

June was following my gaze. I felt self-conscious, fraudulent, as I reached for my notebook and ballpoint. We had agreed that I would write about her life. Reasonably enough, she had in mind a biography, and that was what I had originally intended. But once I had made a start it began to take on another form—not a biography, not even a memoir really, more a divagation; she would be central, but it would not only be about her.

Last time, the snapshot had been a useful point of departure. She was watching me, waiting to begin, as I looked at it. Her elbow was propped on her midriff, and her forefinger rested on the long curve of her chin. The question I really wanted to ask was, How did you get from that face to this, how did you end up looking so extraordinary—was it the life? My, how you've changed!

Instead I said, keeping my eyes on the photograph, 'Bernard's life seems to have been a steady progression, building on what he has, whereas yours seems to have been a long transformation . . .'

Unfortunately, June took this to be a question about Bernard. 'Do you know what he wanted to talk about when he came last month? Eurocommunism! He'd met some Italian delegation the week before. Fat villains in suits banqueting at other people's expense. He said he felt optimistic!' She nodded at the photograph. 'Jeremy, he was actually excited! Just as we were back then. Progression is too kind. Stasis, I'd say. Stagnation.'

She knew this was inaccurate. Bernard had left the party years ago, he had been a Labour MP, he was an Establishment man, a member of its liberal rump, with service on government committees on broadcasting, the environment, pornography. What June really objected to in Bernard was his rationalism. But I did not want to go into that now. I wanted my question answered, the one I had not spoken aloud. I pretended to agree.

'Yes, it's hard to imagine you excited by something like that now.'

She tilted her head back and closed her eyes, her posture for delving at length. We had been over this more than once before, how and why June changed her life. Each time it came out a little differently.

'Are we ready? I spent all the summer of 1938 staying with a family in France, just outside Dijon. Believe it or not, they were actually in the mustard business. They taught me how to cook, and that there is no better place on the planet than France, one youthful conviction I've never been able to revise. When I got back it was my eighteenth birthday and I was given a bicycle, a new one, a beauty. Cycling clubs were still the fashion then, so I joined one, the Socialist Cycling Club of Amersham. Perhaps the idea was to give my stuffy parents a shock, though I don't remember any objections. At weekends about twenty of us would take picnics and pedal along the lanes in the Chilterns, or down the escarpment toward Thame and Oxford. Our club had links with other clubs, and some of these had affiliations with the Communist party. I don't know if there was a plan, a conspiracy, someone should do some research on it. It was probably quite informal, the way it worked out, that these clubs became a recruiting ground for new members. No one ever lectured me. No one was bending my ear. I simply found myself among people I liked, cheerful and bright, and the talk was as you'd imagine —what was wrong with England, the injustices and suffering, how it could be put right, and how these things were being set to rights in the Soviet Union. What Stalin was doing, what Lenin had said, what Marx and Engels wrote. And then there was the gossip. Who was in the party, who had actually been to Moscow, what joining was like, who was thinking of doing it, and so on.

'Now all this talk, all the chatter and giggling took place

as we rode our bikes through the countryside, or sat on those lovely hills with our sandwiches, or stopped by village pub gardens to drink our halves of shandy. Right from the start, the party and all it stood for, all that mumbo-jumbo about the common ownership of the means of production, the historically and scientifically ordained inheritance of the proletariat, the withering away of the whatever, all that fandangle, was associated in my mind with beechwoods, cornfields, sunlight, and barreling down those hills, down those lanes that were tunnels in summer. Communism and my passion for the countryside, as well as my interest in one or two nice-looking boys in shorts—they were all mixed in, and yes, I was very excited.'

As I wrote I wondered, ungenerously, if I was being used —as a conduit, a medium for the final fix June wanted to put on her life. This thought made me less uncomfortable about not writing the biography she wanted.

June continued. She had this worked out rather well.

'That was the beginning. Eight years later I finally joined. And as soon as I did, it was the end, the beginning of the end.'

'The dolmen.'

'Quite so.'

We were about to leapfrog eight years, across the war, from '38 to '46. This was how these conversations went.

On their way back through France in 1946, toward the end of their honeymoon, Bernard and June took a long walk in the Languedoc across a dry limestone plateau called the Causse de Larzac. They came across an ancient burial site known as the Dolmen de la Prunarède a mile or so outside the village where they intended to stay the night. The dolmen stands on a hill, near the edge of the gorge of the River Vis, and the couple sat there for an hour or two in the early evening, facing north toward the Cévennes mountains, talking about the future. Since then we have all been at various times. In 1971 Jenny courted a local boy there, a deserter from the French army. We picnicked there with Bernard and our babies in the mid-eighties. Jenny and I went there once to thrash out a marital problem. It is also a good place to be alone. It has become a family site. Most typically, a dolmen consists of a horizontal slab of weather-worn rock propped on two others to make a low table of stone. There are scores of them up on the Causses, but only one of them is 'the dolmen.'

'What did you talk about?'

She flapped her hand querulously. 'Don't interrogate me. I had a thought then, something I wanted to connect. Ah yes, I have it. The point about the cycling club was that communism and my love of the countryside were inseparable—I suppose they were all part of those romantic, idealistic feelings you have at that age. And now here I was in France in another landscape, far more beautiful in its way than the Chilterns, grander, wilder, even a little frightening. And I was with the man I loved and we were rabbiting on about how we were going to help change the world, and we were on our way home to start our lives together. I even remember thinking to myself, I've never been happier than this. This is it!

'But, you know, there was something wrong, there was a shadow. As we sat there, and the sun went down and the light became quite glorious, I was thinking, But I don't want to go home, I think I'd rather stay here. The more I looked across the gorge, across the Causse de Blandas toward the mountains, the more I realized the obvious—that set against the age and beauty and power of those rocks, politics was a piddling thing. Mankind was a recent event. The universe was indifferent to the fate of the proletariat! I felt frightened. I'd clung to politics all my short adult life—it had given me my friends, my husband, my ideas. I'd been longing to be back in England, and here I was telling myself I'd rather stay and be uncomfortable in this wilderness.

'Bernard was talking on, and no doubt I was chipping in. But I was confused. Perhaps I was not up to any of this, politics or wilderness. Perhaps what I really needed was a nice home and a baby to look after. I was very confused.'

'So you—'

'I haven't finished. There was something else. I had these unsettling thoughts, but I *was* happy at the dolmen. I wanted nothing more than to sit in silence and watch the mountains turning red and breathe in that silky evening air, and to know that Bernard was doing the same, feeling the same. So here was another problem. No stillness, no silence. We were fretting about—who knows—the treachery of reformist social democrats, the condition of the urban poor—people we did not know, people we were in no position at that moment to help. Our lives had gathered to this supreme moment—a sacred site more than five thousand years old, our love for each other, the light, the great space in front of us—and yet we were unable to grasp it, we couldn't draw it into ourselves. We couldn't free ourselves into the present. Instead we wanted to think about setting other people free.

We wanted to think about their unhappiness. We used their wretchedness to mask our own. And our wretchedness was our inability to take the simple good things life was offering us and be glad to have them. Politics, idealistic politics, is all about the future. I've spent my life discovering that the moment you enter the present fully, you find infinite space, infinite time, call it God if you want . . .'

She lost her thread and trailed away. It was not God she was wanting to talk about, it was Bernard. She remembered.

'Bernard thinks that attending to the present is self-indulgence. But that's nonsense. Has he ever sat in silence and thought about his life, or the effect his life has had on Jenny's? Or why he is incapable of living alone and has to have this woman, this 'housekeeper' looking after him? He's completely invisible to himself. He's got facts and figures, his phone is ringing all day, he's always rushing off to give a speech, be on a panel, or whatever. But he never reflects. He's never known a single moment's awe for the beauty of creation. He hates silence, so he knows nothing. I'm answering your question: how could someone so in demand be stagnating? By skidding around on the surface, blathering all day about how things might be if they were ordered better, and learning nothing essential, that's how.'

She fell back against the pillows, exhausted. The long face tilted toward the ceiling. Her breathing was pronounced. We had talked about the evening at the dolmen a number of times, usually as a prelude to the important confrontation the following day. She was angry, and the fact that she knew that I could see she was would be making her angrier still. She had drifted out of control. She knew her account of Bernard's life—the TV appearances, the radio panel discussions, the public man—was ten years out of date. No one heard much from Bernard Tremaine these days. He stayed at home and worked quietly on his book. Only family and a few old friends phoned him now. A woman who lived in the same building came in three hours a day to clean and cook. June's jealousy of her was painful to witness. The ideas by which June lived her life were also the ones by which she measured the distance between Bernard and herself, and if these ideas were powered by a pursuit of the truth, then part of that truth was a bitterness, a disappointment in love. The inaccuracies and exaggerations gave so much away.

I wanted to say something that would make her feel that I was not repelled or dismayed. On the contrary, I warmed to her. I took comfort in June's agitation, in the knowledge that relationships, entanglements, the heart, still mattered, that the old life and the old troubles went on, and that toward the end there was no overview, no grave-cold detachment.

I offered to make her tea and she assented by lifting a finger off the sheet. I crossed to the handbasin to fill the kettle. Outside, the rain had stopped but the wind still blew, and a tiny woman in a pale blue cardigan was making her way across the lawn with the aid of a walking frame. A strong gust could have carried her away. She arrived at a flower bed against a wall and knelt down before her frame, as though at a portable altar. When she was down on the grass on her knees, she maneuvered the frame to one side and took from one pocket in her cardigan a teaspoon and from the other a handful of bulbs. She set about digging holes and pressing the bulbs into them. A few years ago I would have seen no

point at all in planting at her age, I would have watched the
scene and read it as an illustration of futility. Now I could
only watch.

I took the cups to the bedside. June sat up and sipped the
scalding tea soundlessly, in the manner, she once told me,
she had been shown by a deportment teacher at school. She
was away in her thoughts and clearly not yet ready to talk
again. I stared at my pages of notes, amending symbols here
and there to make the shorthand legible. I resolved to visit
the dolmen the next time I was in France. I could walk from
the *bergerie,* ascending by the Pas de l'Azé onto the Causse
and walking north for four or five hours—exquisite in spring
when the wildflowers are out, when whole fields are covered
with orchids. I would sit on that stone and look at that view
again and think about my subject.

Her eyelids were flickering, and in the time it took to
rescue the cup and saucer from her drooping hand and set it
down on the locker she was asleep. These sudden dozes, she
insisted, were not due to exhaustion. They were part of her
condition, a neurological dysfunction that made for an imbal-
ance in the secretion of dopamine. Apparently these narco-
leptic states were numbing and irresistible. It was like having
a blanket thrown over your face, she told me. But when I
mentioned the matter to June's doctor he stared at me and
shook his head infinitesimally, his denial being also a suggestion that I play along. 'She's ill,' he said, 'and she's tired.'

Her breathing had settled to a shallow panting; the wrinkle tree on her forehead was starker, less complex, as though
winter had stripped its boughs. Her empty cup partly ob-

scured the photograph. What transformations! I was still young enough to be amazed by them. There in its frame, the unwritten-on skin, the pretty round head nestling against Bernard's upper arm. I had known them only in later life, but I felt something like nostalgia for the brief, remote time when Bernard and June had been lovingly, uncomplicatedly together. Before the fall. This too contributed to the photograph's innocence—their ignorance of how much and for how long they would be addicted to and irritated by each other. June by Bernard's dreary spiritual impoverishment and 'fundamental lack of seriousness,' his blinkered reasonableness, and by his arrogant insistence, 'against all the accumulating evidence,' that sensible social engineering would deliver mankind from its miseries, from its capacity for cruelty; and Bernard by June's betrayal of her social conscience, her 'self-protecting fatalism' and her 'unbounded credulousness'—how pained he had been by the lengthening roll call of June's certainties: unicorns, wood spirits, angels, mediums, self-healing, the collective unconscious, the 'Christ within us.'

I once asked Bernard about his first meeting with June, during the war. What had drawn him to her? He remembered no first encounter. He became only gradually aware, during the early months of 1944, that a young woman came to his office in Senate House once or twice a week to deliver documents translated from French and to pick up more work to take away. Everyone in Bernard's office could read French, and the material was low-level stuff. He could not see the point of her, therefore he did not see her. She did not exist. Then he overheard someone saying that she was beautiful, and the next time he took a closer look. He began to feel disappointed on the days she did not appear, and foolishly happy when she did. When at last he engaged her in faltering small talk, he found that she was easy to get along with. He had assumed that a beautiful woman was bound to resent talking to a gangling man with big ears. She actually seemed to like him. They had lunch together in the Joe Lyons café on the Strand, where he disguised his nervousness by talking loudly about socialism, and insects—he was something of an amateur entomologist. Later he astounded his colleagues by persuading her to go with him one evening to a film—no, he could not remember which—at a theater in the Haymarket, where he found the courage to kiss her—on the back of her hand first, as though parodying an old-fashioned romance, next on her cheek, and then on her lips, an accelerating, vertiginous progression, the whole thing, from small talk to the first chaste kisses, taking less than four weeks.

June's account: her work as an interpreter and occasional translator of official documents from the French took her one boring afternoon to a corridor in Senate House. She passed the open door of an office next to the one where she had her business and saw a rangy young man with a strange face sprawled uncomfortably on a wooden chair, feet on desk, intent on what looked like a very serious book. He glanced up, held her gaze for a moment, and returned to his reading, already oblivious to her. She lingered for as long as she could without seeming rude—a matter of seconds—and stared, ogled, while pretending to consult the manila folder in her hand. Most of the young men she had been out with she had come to like by overcoming an indefinable distaste. This one she was attracted to immediately. He was 'her type' —now she understood this irritating phrase from the inside. He was obviously clever—everyone in that office was—and she liked the awkward helplessness of his size, and his big, generous face, and the challenging fact that he had looked at her without taking her in. Very few men did that.

She found pretexts for visiting the room where he worked. She delivered items that should have been taken by one of the other girls in her office. In order to lengthen her stay, and because Bernard would not look in her direction, she was forced to develop a flirtation with one of his colleagues, a sad fellow from Yorkshire with spots and a high-pitched voice. She once bumped Bernard's desk in order to spill his tea. He frowned and dabbed at the puddle with his handkerchief without interrupting his reading. She brought him packages intended for elsewhere. He politely put her right. The Yorkshireman wrote a pained declaration of loneliness. He did not expect her to marry him, he said, although he was not ruling that out. But he did hope they would become the closest of friends, like brother and sister. She knew she had to act quickly.

The day she summoned her courage and strode into the office determined to make Bernard take her out to lunch was also the day that he chose to take his first good look at her. His stare was so naked, so guilelessly predatory, that she faltered on her way to his desk. In the corner her would-be brother was grinning and lurching to his feet. June put down her parcel and ran. But now she knew she had her man; now, whenever she walked in, Bernard's big jaw wobbled as he tried to think of something conversational. Lunch at Joe Lyons required only the gentlest of prompts.

It seems odd to me that they never compared memories of those earliest days. Certainly June would have enjoyed the differences. They would have confirmed her later prejudices:

Bernard unreflective, ignorant of the subtle currents that composed the reality he insisted he understood and controlled. However, I resisted communicating Bernard's story to June, or June's to Bernard. It was my decision rather than theirs to keep the accounts confidentially separate. Neither could quite believe this was really the case, and in our conversations I was aware of being used as a bearer of messages and impressions. June would have liked me to scold Bernard on her behalf—for his world view, no less, and for his fast life of radio discussions and housekeeper. Bernard would have liked me to convey to June not only the illusion that he was perfectly intact without her, but also his fondness for her, despite her evident madness, thereby saving him another terrifying visit, or softening the ground for his next. On seeing me, each tried to fish, to wheedle information by drawing me out, usually by offering contestable propositions thinly disguised as questions. Thus Bernard: Have they still got her under sedation? Did she rant nonstop about me? Do you think she'll always hate me? And June: Did he go on about Mrs. Briggs (the housekeeper)? Has he dropped his plans for suicide?

I was evasive. There was nothing I could say that would give satisfaction, and besides, they could have phoned or seen each other anytime they wanted. Like young, absurdly proud lovers, they restrained themselves, believing that the one who called was revealing a weakness, a contemptible emotional dependency.

June woke from a five-minute doze to find a balding man of severe expression sitting by her bed, notebook in hand. Where was she? Who was this person? What did he want?

That widening, panicky surprise in her eyes communicated itself to me, constricting my responses so that I could not immediately find the reassuring words, and stumbled over them when I did. But already, before I had finished, she had the lines of causality restored to her, she had her story again, and she had remembered that her son-in-law had come to record it.

She cleared her throat. 'Where was I?' We both knew she had peeped into the pit, into a chasm of meaninglessness where everything was nameless and without relation, and it had frightened her. It had frightened us both. We could not acknowledge this, or rather, I could not until she had.

By now she knew where she was, just as she knew what came next. But in the brief psychic drama that attended her waking I found myself preparing to resist the inevitable prompt—'the next day.' I wanted to steer her somewhere else. We had been over 'the next day' a half-dozen times. It was family lore, a story burnished with repetition, no longer remembered so much as incanted, like a prayer got by heart. I had heard of it in Poland years before, when I had met Jenny. I had heard it often enough from Bernard, who was not, in the strictest sense, a witness. It had been reenacted at Christmases and other family gatherings. As far as June was concerned, it was to be the centerpiece of my memoir, just as it was in her own story of her life—the defining moment, the experience that redirected, the revealed truth by whose light all previous conclusions had to be rethought. It was a story whose historical accuracy was of less significance than the function it served. It was a myth, all the more powerful for being upheld as documentary. June had persuaded herself that 'the next day' explained everything—why she left the party, why she and Bernard fell into a lifetime's disharmony, why she reconsidered her rationalism, her materialism, how she came to live the life she did, where she lived it, what she thought.

As the family outsider, I was both beguiled and skeptical. Turning points are the inventions of storytellers and dramatists, a necessary mechanism when a life is reduced to, traduced by a plot, when a morality must be distilled from a sequence of actions, when an audience must be sent home with something unforgettable to mark a character's growth. Seeing the light, the moment of truth, the turning point— surely we borrow these from Hollywood or the Bible to make retroactive sense of an overcrowded memory. June's 'black dogs.' Sitting here at the bedside, notebook in my lap, privileged with a glimpse of her void, sharing in the vertigo, I found these almost nonexistent animals too comforting. There would have been too much security in another rehearsal of this famous anecdote.

She must have slipped down the bed while she was dozing. She made an effort to sit upright, but her wrists were too weak, and her hands found no purchase in the bedclothes. I started to rise and help her, but she put me off with a noise, a growl, and rolled onto her side to face me and wedged her head against the folded corner of a pillow.

I began slowly. Was I being mischievous? The thought troubled me, but I had already begun. 'Don't you think the world should be able to accommodate your way of looking at things and Bernard's? Isn't it for the best if some journey inward while others concern themselves with improving the world? Isn't diversity what makes a civilization?'

This last rhetorical question was one too many for June.

The frown of neutral attention disappeared in her hoot of laughter. She could no longer bear to be lying down. She struggled up, successfully this time, into a sitting position while speaking to me through gasps.

'Jeremy, you're a dear old fruit, but you do talk such twaddle. You try too hard to be decent, and have everyone like you and like each other . . . There!'

She was upright at last. The leathery gardener's hands lay clasped together on the sheet, and she stared at me with repressed glee. Or maternal pity. 'So why *hasn't* the world improved? All this free health care and rising wages and cars and TVs and electric toothbrushes per household. Why aren't people content? Isn't there something lacking in these improvements?'

Now that I was being mocked, I felt free. My tone was a little rough. 'So the modern world's a spiritual desert? Even if the cliché is true, what about you, June? Why aren't you happy? Every time I come you show me how bitter you still are about Bernard. Why can't you let it rest? What does it matter now? Let him go. The fact that you haven't or can't doesn't say much for your methods.'

Had I gone too far? While I was speaking June stared across the room toward the window. The silence was ruffled by her protracted intake of breath; then a tighter silence still, followed by a noisy exhalation. She looked straight at me.

'It's true. Of course it's true . . .' She paused before making up her mind to say, 'Everything I've ever done of any value I've had to do alone. I didn't mind at the time. I was content—and by the way, I don't expect to be happy. Happiness is an occasional, summer-lightning thing. But I did find peace of mind, and during all those years I used to think I was all right on my own. I had family, friends, visitors. I was glad when they came, and I was glad when they left. But now . . .'

I had needled her out of reminiscence into confession. I turned a fresh page in my notebook.

'When I was told how ill I was and I came here to seal myself off for one last time, solitude began to look like my biggest single failure. A huge mistake. Making a good life—where's the point in doing that alone? When I think over those years in France, I sometimes feel a cold wind blowing back in my face. Bernard thinks I'm a silly occultist, and I think he's a fish-eyed commissar who'd turn in the lot of us if it would buy a material heaven on earth—that's the family story, the family joke. The truth is we love each other, we've never stopped, we're obsessed. And we failed to do a thing with it. We couldn't make a life. We couldn't give up the love, but we wouldn't bend to its power. The problem's easy enough to describe, but we never described it at the time. We never said, Look, this is how we feel, so where do we go from here? No, it was always muddle, arguments, arrangements about the children, day-to-day chaos and growing separation and different countries. Shutting it all out was how I found peace. If I'm bitter, it's because I haven't forgiven myself. If I'd learned to levitate a hundred feet in the air, it wouldn't have made up for the fact that I never learned how to talk to or be with Bernard. Whenever I'm complaining about some latest social breakdown in the newspapers, I have to remind myself—why should I expect millions of strangers with conflicting interests to get along when I couldn't make a simple society with the father of my children, the man I've loved and remained married to? And there's another thing. If I go on sniping at Bernard, it's because you're here and I know you see him from time to time and—I shouldn't say this—you remind me of him. You don't have his political ambitions, thank God, but there's a dryness and distance about both of you that infuriates and attracts me. And . . .'

She withheld the thought and melted back into the pillows. Since I was supposed to consider myself to have been complimented, I felt constrained by a degree of politeness, a formal requirement to accept what had been offered. There was one word in her confession I wanted to return to as soon as possible. But first, ritual niceties to be dispatched.

'I hope my visits don't upset you, then.'

'I like it when you come.'

'And you'll tell me if you think I'm being too personal.'

'You can ask me anything you want.'

'I don't want to intrude on your . . .'

'I said you can ask me anything you want. If I don't want to answer, then I won't.'

Permission granted. I thought she knew, shrewd old bird, where my attention had snagged. She was waiting for me.

'You say that you and Bernard were . . . obsessed with each other. Do you mean, well, physically . . .'

'Such a typical member of your generation, Jeremy. And getting old enough to start sounding coy about it. Yes, sex, I'm talking about sex.'

I had never heard her use the word. In her BBC wartime broadcast voice she constricted the vowel conspicuously, almost to a 'six.' It sounded crude, quite obscene, on her lips. Was it because she had to force herself to utter it, then repeat it to overcome her distaste? Or was she right? Was I, a sixties man, though always a fastidious one, beginning to choke on the feast?

June and Bernard, sexually obsessed. Since I had only ever known them elderly and hostile, I would have liked to tell her that, like a child with the blasphemous notion of the Queen on the lavatory, I found it hard to imagine.

But instead I said, 'I think I can understand that.'

'I don't think so,' she said, pleased with her certainty. 'You can have no idea what it was like then.'

Even as she was speaking, images and impressions were tumbling through space like Alice, or like the detritus she overtakes, down through a widening cone of time: a smell of office dust; corridor walls painted in cream and brown gloss; everyday items from typewriters to cars, well made and heavy and painted black; unheated rooms, suspicious landladies; farcically solemn young men in baggy flannels biting on pipes; food without herbs or garlic or lemon juice or wine; a constant fiddling with cigarettes, considered a mode of eroticism; and everywhere authority with its bossy, uncompromising Latinate directives on bus tickets and forms and hand-painted signs whose solitary fingers pointed the way through a serious world of brown and black and gray. It was a junk shop exploding in slow motion, my idea of what it was like then, and I was glad June could not sense it too, for I saw no place for sexual obsession.

'Before I met Bernard I'd been out with one or two other young chaps because they had seemed "quite nice." Early on I used to take them home to meet my parents for the judgment: were they "presentable"? I was always measuring men up for possible husbands. That's what my friends did, that was what we talked about. Desire never really came into it, not my own anyway. There was only a vague general sort of longing for a friend who was a man, for a house, a baby, a kitchen—the elements were inseparable. As for the man's feelings, that was a question of how far you let him go. We used to huddle up and talk about it a great deal. If you were going to be married, sex was the price you must pay. After the wedding. It was a tough bargain, but reasonable enough. You couldn't have something for nothing.

'And then, everything changed. Within days of meeting Bernard my feelings were . . . well, I thought I was going to explode. I wanted him, Jeremy. It was like a pain. I didn't want a wedding or a kitchen, I wanted this man. I had lurid fantasies about him. I couldn't talk to my girlfriends honestly. They would have been shocked. Nothing had prepared me for this. I urgently wanted sex with Bernard, and I was terrified. I knew that if he asked, if he insisted, I would have no choice. And it was obvious that his feelings were intense too. He wasn't the kind to make demands, but one afternoon, for a set of reasons I've now forgotten, we found ourselves alone in a house belonging to the parents of a girlfriend of mine. I think it had something to do with the fact that it was raining very hard. We went up to the guest bedroom and started to undress. I was about to have what I had been thinking about for weeks, but I was miserable, full of dread, as if I were being led off to my own execution . . .'

She caught my quizzical look—why misery?—and drew an impatient breath.

'What your generation doesn't know, and mine has almost forgotten, is how ignorant we were still, how bizarre attitudes were then—to sex, and all that went with it. Contraception, divorce, homosexuality, VD. And pregnancy outside marriage was unthinkable, the very worst possible thing. In the twenties and thirties respectable families were locking their pregnant daughters away in mental institutions. Unmarried mothers were marched through the streets, humiliated by the organizations that were supposed to be looking after them. Girls killed themselves trying to abort. It looks like madness now, but in those days a pregnant girl was likely to feel that everyone was right and that *she* was mad and deserved everything she got. Official attitudes were so punitive, so harsh. There was no financial support, of course. An unmarried mother was an outcast, a disgrace, dependent on vengeful charities, church groups or whatever. We all knew a half-dozen terrible, cautionary tales to keep us on the straight and narrow. They weren't enough that afternoon, but I certainly thought I was fixing my doom as we went up the stairs to this tiny room at the top of the house where the wind and the rain were beating at the window, just like today. We had no precautions, of course, and in my ignorance I thought pregnancy was inevitable. And I knew that I was not able to turn back. I was miserable about it, but I was also tasting freedom. It was the freedom I imagine a criminal must experience, even if only for a moment, as he sets about his crime. I'd always done more or less what people expected of me, but now I knew myself for the first time. And I simply had to— had to, Jeremy—get close up to this man . . .'

I cleared my throat softly. 'And, um, how was it?' I could not credit that I was asking June Tremaine this question. Jenny would never believe me.

June gave another of her hoots. I had never seen her so animated. 'It was a surprise! Bernard was the clumsiest of creatures, always spilling his drink or banging his head on a beam. Lighting someone's cigarette was an ordeal for him. I was sure I was the first girl he'd been with. He hinted otherwise, but that was just the form, that was what he was supposed to say. So I rather thought we'd be babes in the wood together, and I honestly didn't mind. I wanted him on any terms. We climbed into this narrow bed, me giggling with terror and excitement, and would you believe it—Bernard was a genius! All the words you'd find in a romantic novel—gentle, strong, skillful—and, well, *inventive*. When we'd finished he did this ridiculous thing. He suddenly leaped up and ran to the window, threw it open to the storm, and stood there naked, long and thin and white, beating his chest and yodeling like Tarzan while leaves came swirling in. It was so stupid! D'you know, he made me laugh so hard that I widdled on the bed. We had to turn the mattress over. Then we picked hundreds of leaves off the carpet. I took the sheets home in a shopping bag and washed them and got them back on the bed with my friend's help. She was a year older than me and so disgusted that she didn't speak to me for months!'

Experiencing in myself something of June's criminal freedom of forty-five years ago, I was close to bringing up the matter of the size Bernard 'took.' Was it merely, as now seemed the case, June's occasional slander? Or the paradoxical secret of his success? Or again, when he was so long in the body, wasn't this simply an error of relative judgment? But there are things one may not ask one's mother-in-law, and besides, she was frowning, trying to formulate.

'It might have been a week later that Bernard came home and met my parents, and I'm almost certain that was the time he knocked a full teapot over the Wilton. Apart from that he was a success, perfectly appropriate—public school,

Cambridge, a nice shy way of talking to his elders. So we began a double life. We were the darling young couple who gladdened all hearts by engaging to be married as soon as the war was over. At the same time, we continued what we had started. There were unused rooms in Senate House and other government buildings. Bernard was clever at getting hold of keys. In summer, there were the beech woods around Amersham. It was an addiction, a madness, a secret life. We were taking precautions, by then, but quite honestly by that time I couldn't have cared less.

'Whenever we talked about the world beyond ourselves, we talked about communism. It was our other obsession. We decided to forgive the party its stupidity at the beginning of the war, and to join as soon as there was peace and we had left our jobs. Marx, Lenin, Stalin, the way forward—we agreed on everything. A fine union of bodies and minds! We'd founded a private utopia, and it was only a matter of time before the nations of the world followed our example. These were the months that shaped us. Behind all our frustration over all these years has been the wish to get back to those happy days. Once we began to see the world differently, we could feel time running out on us and we were impatient with each other. Every disagreement was an interruption of what we knew was possible—and soon there was only interruption. And in the end time did run out, but the memories are still there, accusing us, and we still can't let each other alone.

'One thing I learned that morning after the dolmen was that I had courage, physical courage, and that I could stand alone. That's a significant discovery for a woman, or it was in my day. Perhaps it was a fateful discovery too, a disastrous one. I'm not so sure now I *should* have stood alone. The rest is harder to tell, especially to a skeptic like yourself.'

I was about to protest, but she waved me down.

'I'm going to say it again anyway. I'm getting tired. You'll have to go soon. And I want to go over the dream again too. I want to be sure you've got that right.'

She hesitated, gathering strength for the one last talking bout of the afternoon.

'I know that everyone thinks I've made too much of it—a young girl frightened by a couple of dogs on a country path. But you wait until you come to make sense of your life. You'll either find you're too old and lazy to make the attempt, or you'll do what I've done, single out a certain event, find in something ordinary and explicable a means of expressing what might otherwise be lost to you—a conflict, a change of heart, a new understanding. I'm not saying these animals were anything other than what they appeared to be. Despite what Bernard says, I don't actually believe they were Satan's familiars, hellhounds or omens from God or whatever he tells people I believe. But there is a side of the story he doesn't care to emphasize. Next time you see him, get him to tell you what the *Maire* of St. Maurice told us about those dogs. He'll remember. It was a long afternoon on the terrace of the Hôtel des Tilleuls. I haven't mythologized these animals. I've made use of them. They set me free. I discovered something.'

She pushed her hand out across the sheet toward me. I could not quite bring myself to stretch out my own hand and take hers. Some journalistic impulse, some queer notion of neutrality, prevented me. As she talked on, and I continued to transcribe in the dashing arabesques of my shorthand, I felt myself to be weightless, empty-headed, suspended in my uncertainty between two points, the banal and the profound; I did not know which I was hearing. Embarrassed, I hunched over my writing so that I did not have to meet her eye.

'I met evil and discovered God. I call it my discovery, but of course it's nothing new, and it's not mine. Everyone has to make it for himself. People use different language to describe it. I suppose all the great world religions began with individuals making inspired contact with a spiritual reality and then trying to keep that knowledge alive. Most of it gets lost in rules and practices and addiction to power. That's how religions are. In the end, though, it hardly matters how you describe it once the essential truth has been grasped—that we have within us an infinite resource, a potential for a higher state of being, a goodness . . .'

I had heard this before, in one form or another, from a spiritually inclined headmaster, a dissident vicar, an old girlfriend returning from India, from Californian professionals and dazed hippies. She saw me shifting in my seat, but she pressed on.

'Call it God, or the spirit of love, or the Atman or the Christ or the laws of nature. What I saw that day, and on many days since, was a halo of colored light around my body. But the appearance is irrelevant. What matters is to make the connection with this center, this inner being, and then extend and deepen it. Then carry it outward, to others. The healing power of love . . .'

The memory of what happened next still pains me. I could not help myself, my discomfort was simply too intense. I could not bear to hear any more. Perhaps the years of my loneliness were the culture that nourished my skepticism, my protection against those clarion calls to love, to improve, to yield up the defensible core of selfhood and see it dissolve in the lukewarm milk of universal love and goodness. It is the kind of talk that makes me blush. I wince for those who speak this way. I don't see it, I don't believe it.

Mumbling an excuse about leg cramp, I got to my feet, but too quickly. My chair tipped backward and smacked against the cupboard with a loud crack. I was the one who was startled. She was watching me, slightly amused, as I began to apologize for the interruption.

She said, 'I know. The words are tired, and so am I. Another time it would be better if I could show you what I mean. Another time . . .' She did not have the strength to move against my disbelief. The afternoon was at an end.

I was trying again to apologize for my rudeness, and she spoke over me. Her tone was light enough, but it could well have been that she was offended.

'Would you mind rinsing out those teacups before you go. Thank you, Jeremy.'

As I stood at the washbasin with my back to her, I heard her sigh as she settled deeper into the bed. Outside, the branches were still shaking in the wind. I felt a momentary pleasure that I would be rejoining the world, letting the westerly wind blow me back to London, into my present, out of her past. While I dried the cups and saucers and returned them to the shelf, I tried to frame a better apology for my rude behavior. The soul, an afterlife, a universe filled with meaning: it was the very comfort this glad-hearted believing gave that pained me; conviction and self-interest were too tightly entwined. How could I tell her that?

When I turned back toward her, her eyes were closed and her breathing was in its shallow rhythm. But she was not yet asleep. As I was gathering up my bag from near her bed, she murmured without opening her eyes, 'I wanted to go over the dream again.'

It was in my notebook, the short, unvarying, presleep dream that had haunted her for forty years. Two dogs are running down a path into the gorge. The larger leaves a trail of blood, easily visible on the white stones. June knows that the mayor of a nearby village has not sent out his men to track the animals down. They descend into the shadow cast by the high cliffs, down into the thickets, and up the other side. She sees them again, across the gorge, heading into the mountains, and even though they are going far away from her, this is the moment of terror that jolts her; she knows they will return.

I reassured her. 'I've got it down.'

'You need to remember that it comes when I'm still half awake. I actually *see* them, Jeremy.'

'I won't forget.'

She nodded, eyes still closed. 'Can you see yourself out?'

It was almost a joke, an enfeebled irony. I leaned over her and kissed her cheek and whispered in her ear, 'I think I can manage.' Then I went quietly across her room and stepped out into the corridor, onto the swirling red and yellow carpet, thinking, as I always did when I left her, that this would be the last time.

And it was.

She died four weeks later, 'peacefully in her sleep'—so said the senior nurse who phoned Jenny with the news. We did not believe it had been that way, but neither did we want to doubt.

She was buried in the churchyard of the village near Chestnut Reach. We drove down with our children and two of our nephews, and we took Bernard. It was an uncomfortable journey. The day was hot, it was cramped in the car, and there were roadworks and heavy traffic on the motorway. Bernard sat in the front, silent all the way. Sometimes he put his hands over his face for a second or two. Mostly he stared ahead. He did not seem to be crying. Jenny sat in the back with the baby on her lap. At her side the children discussed the death. We sat listening helplessly, unable to steer the conversation away. Alexander, our four-year-old, was aghast that we were planning to put his granny, of whom he was very fond, in a wooden box and lower her into a hole in the ground and cover her with earth.

'She doesn't like that,' he said confidently.

Harry, his seven-year-old cousin, had the facts. 'She's dead, stupid. Stone cold dead. She doesn't know anything about it.'

'When is she coming back?'

'Never. You don't come back when you're dead.'

'But when *is* she?'

'Never ever ever ever. She's in heaven, stupid.'

'When is she coming back? Granddad? When is she, Granddad?'

It was a relief that in such a remote place the crowd was so large. Along the road from the Norman church dozens of cars were tilted at angles on the grass shoulders. The air above their hot roofs rippled. I was only just beginning to attend funerals regularly, so far exclusively secular affairs for three friends who had died of AIDS. The Anglican service that day was more familiar to me from movies. Like one of the great Shakespeare speeches, the graveside oration, studded in fragments in the memory, was a succession of brilliant phrases, book titles, dying cadences that breathed life, pure alertness, along the spine. I was watching Bernard. He stood on the vicar's right, hands straight down at his sides, staring forward as he had in the car, keeping himself well under control.

After the service I saw him detach himself from June's old friends and wander off among the headstones, stopping here and there to read one, and go toward a yew tree. He stood in its shade, resting his elbows on the graveyard wall. I was going toward him to say the few clumsy sentences I had half prepared when I heard him call June's name over the wall. I went closer and saw that he was sobbing. He leaned his long thin body forward, then straightened again. Up and down he bobbed in the shade as he cried. I turned away, guilty at my intrusion, and hurried back, passing two men filling in the grave, to catch up with the chattering crowd, its sadness fading in the summery air as it wound its way out of the graveyard, along the road, past the parked cars, toward the entrance to a field of unmowed grass, in the center of which stood a creamy marquee, its sides rolled up for the heat. Behind me, dry earth and stones chinked against the sextons' shovels. Ahead, this was how June must have imagined it: children playing in and out of the guy ropes, waiters in starched white jackets serving drinks from behind trestles draped in sheets, and, already, the first of the guests, a young couple, lolling on the green.

2

. . . .

Berlin

A little more than two years later, six-thirty on a November morning, I woke to discover Jenny in the bed beside me. She had been away ten days in Strasbourg and Brussels and had returned late in the night. We rolled into a sleepy embrace. Minor reunions like this are one of the more exquisite domestic pleasures. She felt both familiar and novel—how easily one gets used to sleeping alone. Her eyes were closed and she half smiled as she fitted her cheek into the space below my collarbone that seemed to have formed itself over the years to her shape. We had at most an hour, probably less, before the children woke to discover her—all the more of a thrill for them because I had been vague about her return in case she did not make the last plane. I reached down and squeezed her buttocks. Her hand moved lightly across my belly. I felt for the homely bump at the base of her pinkie where a sixth finger was amputated shortly after her birth. As many fingers, her mother used to say, as an insect has legs. Some minutes later, which may have been interrupted by a brief doze, we began the companionable lovemaking that is the privilege and compromise of married life.

We were just waking to the urgency of our pleasure, and stirring more vigorously on each other's behalf, when the phone on the bedside table rang. We should have remembered to unplug it. We exchanged a look. In silence we agreed that it was still early enough for a phone call to be unusual, perhaps an emergency.

Sally was the most likely caller. She had come to live with us twice, and the strain on family life had been too great for us to keep her. Several years before, at the age of twenty-one, she had married a man who had beaten her and left her with a child. Two years later, she had been found unfit, too violent, to care for her little boy, who was now with foster parents. She had beaten the alcoholism only to make a second disastrous marriage. She now lived in a hostel in Manchester. Her mother, Jean, was dead, and Sally counted on us for affection and support. She never asked for money. I could never rid myself of the idea that her unhappy life was my responsibility.

Jenny was on her back, so I was the one who leaned across. But it was not Sally, it was Bernard, already halfway through a sentence. He was not talking, he was jabbering. I could hear excited commentary behind him, which gave way to a police siren. I tried to interrupt, calling out his name. The first intelligible thing I heard him say was 'Jeremy, are you listening? Are you still there?'

I felt myself shrinking inside his daughter. I kept a sensible tone. 'Bernard, I didn't catch a word of that. Start again, slowly.'

Jenny was making signs, offering to take the receiver from me. But Bernard had started again. I shook my head and turned my gaze into the pillow.

'Turn your radio on, dear boy. Or the television, even better. They're streaming through. You won't believe it—'

'Bernard, who is streaming through what?'

'I just told you. They're taking down the Wall! It's hard to believe, but I'm watching it now, East Berliners coming through . . .'

My first, selfish thought was that nothing was immediately required of me. I did not have to leave my bed and go out and do something useful. I promised Bernard I would call him back, put the phone down, and told Jenny the news.

'Amazing.'

'Incredible.'

We were doing our best to keep its full importance at arm's length, for we did not yet belong to the world, to the striving community of the fully dressed. An important principle was at stake: that we maintain the primacy of the private life. And so we resumed. But the spell had been broken. Cheering crowds were surging through the early morning gloom of our bedroom. We were both elsewhere.

Finally it was Jenny who said, 'Let's go downstairs and look.'

We stood in the living room in our dressing gowns with mugs of tea, staring at the set. It did not seem right to sit. East Berliners in nylon anoraks and bleached-out jean jackets, pushing buggies or holding their children's hands, were filing past Checkpoint Charlie, unchecked. The camera bobbed and weaved intrusively into wide-armed embraces. A tearful woman, her complexion rendered ghoulish by a single TV spotlight, spread her hands, began to speak, and was too choked up to utter the words. Crowds of West Berliners cheered and thumped good-naturedly on the roof of each brave ludicrous Trabant nosing into freedom. Two sisters clung to each other and wouldn't be parted for an interview. Jenny and I were in tears, and when the children came running in to greet her, the little drama of reunion, the hugs and cuddles on the living room carpet, drew poignancy from the joyful events in Berlin—and made Jenny cry outright.

An hour later Bernard phoned again. It was four years now since he had started to call me 'dear boy,' ever since, I suspected, he had joined the Garrick Club. Such, Jenny maintained, was the distance traveled since 'comrade.'

'Dear boy. I want to get over to Berlin as soon as possible.'

'Good idea,' I said straightaway. 'You should go.'

'Seats are gold dust. Everyone wants to go. I've put a hold on two places on a flight this afternoon. I have to let them know in an hour.'

'Bernard, I'm just off to France.'

'Make a diversion. It's a historic moment.'

'I'll phone you back.'

Jenny was scathing about her father. 'He has to go and

see his Big Mistake put right. He'll need someone to carry his bags.'

When it was put like that, I was ready to say no. But during breakfast, roused by the tinny triumphalism of the black-and-white portable we had balanced by the kitchen sink, I began to feel an impatient excitement, a need for adventure after days of domestic duties. Again the set gave out a miniature roar, and I was feeling like a boy locked out of the stadium on Cup Final day. History was happening, without me.

After the children had been delivered to their playgroup and school, I raised the matter with Jenny again. She was pleased to be back home. She moved from room to room, cordless phone always within reach, tending the houseplants that had wilted under my care.

'Go' was her recommendation. 'Don't listen to me, I'm jealous. But before you go, you'd better finish what you started.'

The best of all possible arrangements. I rerouted my flight to Montpellier through Berlin and Paris and confirmed Bernard's booking. I phoned Berlin to ask my friend Gunter if we could borrow his apartment. I called Bernard to tell him that I would collect him in a taxi at two o'clock. I canceled engagements, left instructions, and packed my bag. On the TV was a half-mile queue of East Berliners outside a bank, waiting for their hundred deutschemarks. Jenny and I returned to the bedroom for an hour, then she left in a hurry for an appointment. I sat in the kitchen in my dressing gown and ate an early lunch of warmed-up leftovers. On the portable, other parts of the Wall had been breached. People were converging on Berlin from all over the planet. A huge party was in the making. Journalists and TV crews could not find hotel rooms. Back upstairs, standing under the shower, invigorated and clarified by lovemaking, bellowing the snatches of Verdi I could remember in Italian, I congratulated myself on my rich and interesting life.

An hour and a half later I left the taxi waiting in Addison Road and sprinted up the flight of steps to Bernard's flat. He was actually standing just inside the open doorway, holding his hat and coat, with his bags at his feet. He had only lately acquired the fussy exactitude of old age, the necessary caution to accommodate a reliably useless memory. I picked up his bags (Jenny was right) and he was about to pull the door shut, but already he was frowning and raising a forefinger.

'One last look around.'

I put the bags down and followed him in, in time to see him scoop up his house keys and passport from the kitchen table. He held them up for me with a told-you-so look, as though I were the one who had forgotten them and he were to be congratulated.

I had shared London cabs with Bernard before. His legs almost reached the partition. We were still in first gear, still pulling away, and Bernard was making a steeple of his fingers under his chin and beginning, 'The point is . . .' His voice did not have June's clipped, wartime mandarin quality; instead, it was pitched slightly high and was overprecise in its enunciation, the way Lytton Strachey's might have been, or Malcolm Muggeridge's was, the way certain educated Welshmen used to talk. If you didn't already know and like Bernard, it could sound affected. 'The point is that German unity is an inevitability. The Russians will rattle their sabers, the French will wave their arms, the British will um and ah. Who knows what the Americans will want, what will suit them best. But none of it matters. The Germans will have unity because they want it and they've provided for it in their constitution and no one can stop them. They'll have it sooner rather than later because no chancellor in his right mind is going to let the glory go to his successor. And they'll have it on West German terms because they're the ones who'll be paying for it.'

He had a way of presenting all his opinions as well-established facts, and his certainties did have a sinuous power. What was required of me was to present another view, whether I believed in it or not. Bernard's habits of private conversation had been formed by years of public debate. A fair bout of adversarial discussion was what would bring us to the truth. As we headed toward Heathrow I obligingly argued that the East Germans might retain attachments to some features of their system and therefore might not be so easy to assimilate, that the Soviet Union had hundreds of thousands of troops in the GDR and could certainly affect the outcome if it wanted, and that marrying the two systems in practical and economic terms could take years.

He nodded in satisfaction. His fingers still supported his chin, and he was waiting patiently for me to finish so that he could set about my arguments. Methodically, he took them in order. The enormous popular momentum against the East German state had reached a stage where lingering attachments would only be discovered too late, in the form of nostalgia. The Soviet Union had lost interest in controlling its eastern satellites; it was no longer a superpower in any but military terms, and it badly needed Western goodwill and German money. As for the practical difficulties of German union, they could be dealt with later, after the political marriage had ensured the Chancellor his place in the history books and a good chance of winning the next election with millions of new and grateful voters.

Bernard was still talking and seemed unaware that the taxi had stopped outside our terminal. I leaned forward and settled the fare while he was addressing at length the third of my points. The driver turned around in his seat and opened his sliding glass door to listen. He was in his fifties, completely bald, with a rubbery, babyish face and large staring eyes of a blazing fluorescent blue.

When Bernard was done he chipped in. 'Yeah, and then what, mate? The Krauts'll start throwing their weight around again. That's when the bother'll start . . .'

Bernard flinched the moment the driver began to speak, and fumbled for his bags. The consequences of German unity were probably the next subject for debate, but instead of being drawn in, even for a condescending minute, Bernard was embarrassed and scrabbling to get out.

'Where's yer stability?' the driver was saying. 'Where's yer balance of power? On your eastern side you got Russia going down the tube and all them little countries, Poland and stuff, deep in the shit with debts and everything—'

'Yes, yes, you're right, it is indeed a worry,' Bernard said as he gained the safety of the pavement. 'Jeremy, we mustn't miss that plane.'

The driver had wound down his window. 'On the west, you got Britain, not a European player is it, not really. Still got its tongue up the American fundament, if you'll pardon my French. Which leaves the French. Christ, the French!'

'Goodbye, and thank you,' Bernard cooed, and was even prepared to seize his own bags and totter with them to open up some distance. I caught up with him by the automatic doors into the terminal. He put his bags down in front of me and rubbed his right hand with his left as he said, 'I simply cannot stand being harangued by cabbies.'

I knew what he meant, but I also thought that Bernard was rather too fastidious about whom he debated with. 'You've lost the common touch.'

'Never had it, dear boy. Ideas were my thing.'

Half an hour after takeoff, we ordered champagne from the drinks cart and toasted freedom. Then Bernard returned to the matter of the common touch.

'Now June had it. She could get along with anybody. She would have taken on that taxi driver. Surprising in someone who ended up a recluse. She was a far better communist than I, really.'

These days, a mention of June sent a little charge of guilt through me. Since her death in July 1987 I had done nothing with the memoir I was supposed to be writing beyond sorting the notes into order and putting them away in a box file. My work (I run a small publishing company specializing in textbooks), family life, a house move last year—the usual excuses did not make me feel easier. Perhaps my trip to France, the *bergerie* and its associations, would set me going again. And there were still things I wanted to know from Bernard.

'I don't think June would think that was much of a compliment.'

Bernard held up his plastic goblet to allow the sunlight

flooding the cabin to be refracted by the champagne. 'These days, who would? But there was a year or two when she was a real tigress for the cause.'

'Until the Gorge de Vis.'

He knew when I was pumping him. He leaned back and smiled without looking at me. 'Is this the life and times we're on now?'

'It's time I did something about it.'

'Did she ever tell you about the row we had? In Provence, on our way home from Italy, at least a week or so before we reached the gorge.'

'I don't think she mentioned it.'

'It was on a railway platform near a little town whose name I don't remember now. We were waiting for a local train to take us into Arles. It was an uncovered station, barely more than a stop really, and terribly smashed up. The waiting room had been burned down. It was hot, there was no shade, and there was nowhere to sit down. We were tired and the train was late. We also had the place to ourselves. Perfect conditions for our first matrimonial set-to.

'At one point I left June standing with our luggage and wandered the length of the platform—you know how one does when time drags—right along to where it ended. The place was a mess. I think a barrel of tar or paint had been spilled. The paving stones had been dislodged and weeds had pushed up and dried out in the heat. At the back, away from the tracks, was a clump of arbutus that had managed somehow to flourish rather well. I was admiring it when I saw a movement on a leaf. I went closer and there it was, a dragonfly, a ruddy darter, *Sympetrum sanguineum,* a male, you know, brilliant red. They're not exactly rare but it was unusually large, a beauty.

'Amazingly I managed to trap it in my cupped hands, then I ran back along the platform to where June was and got her to take it in her hands while I dug into my bag for my traveling kit. I opened it and took out the killing bottle and asked June to bring the creature over to me. She still had her hands cupped, like this, but she was looking at me with an odd expression, a kind of horror. She said, "What are you going to do?" And I said, "I want to take it home." She didn't come closer. She said, "You mean you're going to kill it." "Of course I am," I said. "It's a beauty." She went cold and logical at this point. "It's beautiful, therefore you want to kill it." Now June, as you know, grew up near the countryside and never showed much compunction about killing mice, rats, cockroaches, wasps—anything that got in her way, really. It was jolly hot and this was not the moment to start an ethical discussion about the rights of insects. So I said, "June, do just bring it over here." Perhaps I spoke too roughly. She took half a step away from me, and I could see she was on the point of setting it free. I said, "June, you know how much it means to me. If you let it go, I'll never forgive you." She was struggling with herself. I repeated what I had said, and then she came toward me, extremely sullen, transferred the dragonfly to my hands, and watched me put it in the killing bottle and store it away. She was silent as I put my stuff back in the case, and then, perhaps because she was blaming herself for not setting it free, she flew into an almighty rage.'

The drinks cart was making a second run and Bernard faltered as he decided against ordering a second champagne.

'Like the best of rows, it moved rapidly from the particular to the general. My attitude to this poor creature was typical of my attitude to most other things, including herself. I was cold, theoretical, arrogant. I never showed any emotion, and I prevented her from showing it. She felt watched, analyzed, she felt she was part of my insect collection. All I was interested in was abstraction. I claimed to love "creation," as she called it, but in fact I wanted to control it, choke the life out of it, label it, arrange it in rows. And my politics were another case in point. It wasn't injustice that bothered me so much as untidiness. It wasn't the brotherhood of man that appealed to me so much as the efficient organization of man. What I wanted was a society as neat as a barracks, justified by scientific theories. We were standing there in this ferocious sunlight and she was shouting at me, "You don't even like working-class people! You never speak to them. You don't know what they're like. You loathe them. You just want them arranged in neat rows like your bloody insects!" '

'What did you say?'

'Not a great deal at first. You know how I hate scenes. I kept thinking, I've married this lovely girl and she hates me. What a terrible mistake! And then, because I had to say something, I mounted a defense of my hobby. Most people, I told her, instinctively disliked the insect world, and entomologists were the ones to take notice of it, study its ways and life cycles, and generally care about it. Naming insects, classifying them into groups and subgroups, was an important part of all that. If you learned to name a part of the world, you learned to love it. Killing a few insects was irrelevant against this larger fact. Insect populations were enormous, even in a rare species. They were genetically clones of each other, so it didn't make sense to talk of individuals, still less of their rights. "There you go again," she said. "You're not talking to me at all. You're giving a lecture." That was when I began to get stirred up. As for my politics, I went on, yes, I liked ideas and what was the harm in that? It was for other people to agree or disagree and disprove them. And it was true, I felt awkward with working-class people, but that didn't mean I loathed them. That was absurd. I'd quite understand it if they felt awkward with me. As for my feelings toward her, yes, I wasn't awfully emotional, but that didn't mean I didn't have emotions. It was simply the way I was brought up, and if she wanted to know, I loved her more than I'd ever be able to say and that was that, and if I didn't tell her often enough, well I was sorry for that, but in future I jolly well would, every day if necessary.

'And then an extraordinary thing happened. Actually, two things happened at once. As I was saying all this, our train pulled in with a great clatter and an awful lot of smoke and steam, and just as it came to a stop June burst into tears and threw her arms around me and broke the news that she was pregnant and that holding a little insect in her hands made her feel responsible not only for the life that was growing inside her but for all life, and that letting me kill that beautiful creature was an awful mistake and she was sure that nature would take its revenge and something terrible was going to happen to the baby. The train pulled out and we were still on the platform with our arms round each other. I had half a mind to dance up and down the platform with joy, but like an idiot, I was trying to explain Darwin to June and comfort her by saying that there simply was no place in the scheme of things for the kind of revenge she was talking about, and that nothing would happen to our baby—'

'Jenny.'

'Yes, of course. Jenny.'

Bernard pressed the call button above his head and told the steward that he had changed his mind and we would have the champagne after all. When it came we raised our glasses, it seemed, to the impending birth of my wife.

'After this news we couldn't bear to wait for another train, so we walked into the town—hardly more than a large village really, and I wish I could remember its name—and we found the only hotel and took a huge creaky room on the second floor with a balcony overlooking a small square. Perfect place, and we always meant to go back. June knew the name of it, and I'll never get it now. We stayed there two days, celebrated the baby, took stock of our lives, laid our plans like any young married couple. It was a wonderful reconciliation —and we barely stirred from the room.

'But there was an evening when June had fallen asleep early and I was restless. I went for a stroll round the square, had a couple of drinks in a café. You know how it is when you've been with someone so intensely for hours on end, and then you're on your own again. It's as if you've been in a dream. You come to yourself. I sat outside this bar, watched them playing boules. It was an awfully hot evening, and for the first time I had the chance to think over some of the things June had said at the station. I tried hard to imagine what it would be like to believe, really to believe, that nature could take revenge on a fetus for the death of an insect. She'd been deadly serious about it, to the point of tears. And honestly, I couldn't. It was magical thinking, completely alien to me.'

'But Bernard, don't you ever have that feeling, when you're tempting fate? Don't you ever touch wood?'

'That's just a game, a manner of speaking. We know it's superstition. This belief that life really does have rewards and punishments, that underneath it all there's a deeper pattern of meaning beyond what we give it ourselves—that's all so much consoling magic. Only—'

'Biographers?'

'I was going to say women. Perhaps all I'm saying is that sitting there with my drink in that hot little square, I was beginning to understand something about women and men.'

I wondered what my sensible, efficient wife Jenny would have made of this.

Bernard had finished his champagne and was eyeing the untouched inch or two in my bottle. I gave it to him as he said, 'Let's face it, the physical differences are just the, just the . . .'

'Tip of the iceberg?'

He smiled. 'Thin end of a giant wedge. Anyway, I sat there and had another drink or two. And then, I know it's foolish to give too much weight to what people say to you in anger, but all the same, I brooded on what she had said about my politics, perhaps because there was an element of truth in it, for all of us, and she had said similar things before. I remember thinking, She won't stick in the party long. She's got her own ideas and they're strong and strange.

'All this came back to me this afternoon when I ran away from that cabbie. If it had been June, the June of 1946, not the June who gave up on politics altogether, she would have spent a happy half hour talking European politics with that fellow, putting him on to the right literature, getting his name for the mailing list, and who knows, signing him up. She would have been prepared to miss her plane.'

We lifted our bottles and glasses to make way for the lunch trays.

'Anyway, there it is, for what it's worth—another item for the life and times. She was a better communist than I. But in that outburst of hers at the station you could see a long way ahead. You could see her disaffection with the party coming, and you could see the beginnings of the hocus-pocus that filled her life from then on. It certainly wasn't a sudden matter of one morning down the Gorge de Vis, whatever she liked to say.'

It hurt to hear my own skepticism thrown back at me. As I buttered my frozen roll, I felt drawn to make mischief on June's behalf. 'But Bernard, what about the insect's revenge?'

'What about it?'

'Jenny's sixth finger!'

'Dear boy, what are we going to drink with our lunch?'

We went first to Gunter's apartment in Kreuzberg. I left Bernard waiting in a taxi while I carried our bags across the courtyard and took them up to the fourth-floor landing of the *hinterhaus*. The neighbor across the way, who was keeping the key for me, spoke a little English and knew we were here for the Wall.

'No good,' she insisted. 'Too many people here. In the shop, no milk, no bread, no fruit. In the U-Bahn also. Too many!'

Bernard told the driver to take us to the Brandenburg Gate, but this turned out to be a mistake, and I began to see what Gunter's neighbor meant. There were too many people, too much traffic. The usually busy roads were carrying an extra burden of fuming Wartburgs and Trabants out on their first night of sightseeing. The pavements were crammed. Everyone, East and West Berliners as well as outsiders, was a tourist now. Bands of West Berlin teenagers with beer cans and bottles of sekt passed our trapped car chanting football songs. In the darkness of the rear seat I began to feel a vague regret that I was not already in the *bergerie,* high above St. Privat, preparing the house for winter. Even at this time of year you might still hear the cicadas on a mild evening. Then, remembering Bernard's story on the plane, I deflected my regret with the resolve to get from him what I could while we were here and to revive the memoir.

We gave up on the taxi and walked in. It was twenty minutes to the Victory Monument, and from there, stretching ahead of us, was the broad June 17 approach to the Gate. Someone had tied a piece of cardboard over the street sign and painted NOVEMBER 9TH. Hundreds of people were moving in the same direction. A quarter of a mile away the Brandenburg Gate stood illuminated, looking rather too small, too squat for its global importance. At its base, the darkness appeared to intensify in a wide band. Only when we reached it would we discover that this was the gathering crowd.

Bernard seemed to be hanging back. He held his hands behind his back and leaned forward into an imaginary wind. Everyone was overtaking us.

'When were you last here, Bernard?'

'Do you know, I've never actually walked along here. Berlin? There was a conference on the Wall on its fifth anniversary, in 'sixty-six. Before that, my God! Nineteen fifty-three. We were an unofficial delegation of British communists who came to protest—no, that's too strong—express reverent concern to the East German party about the way they put down the Uprising. There was hell to pay from some of the comrades when we got home.'

Two girls in black leather jackets, skintight jeans, and silver-studded cowboy boots brushed by us. They had linked arms and were not defiant of the glances they were attracting so much as oblivious to them. Their hair was dyed black. The identical ponytails that swung behind them completed a passing reference to the fifties. But not, I imagined, Bernard's fifties. He was watching them go, frowning slightly. He stooped to murmur confidentially into my ear. It was hardly necessary, for there was no one near us, and all around were the sounds of voices and footsteps.

'Ever since she died, I've found myself looking at young girls. Of course, it's pathetic at my age. But it's not their bodies I stare at so much as their faces. I'm looking for a trace of her. It's become a habit. I'm always searching for a gesture, an expression, something about the eyes or the hair, anything that will keep her alive for me. It's not the June you knew that I'm looking for, otherwise I'd be scaring the wits out of old ladies. It's the girl I married . . .'

June in the framed photograph. Bernard rested his hand on my arm.

'There's something else. In the first six months, I couldn't put the idea out of my mind that she would try to communicate with me. Apparently it's a very common thing. Grief breeds superstition.'

'Hardly in your scientific scheme.' I regretted the harsh levity of this remark, but Bernard nodded.

'Exactly so, and as soon as I felt stronger I came to my senses. But for a while I couldn't stop thinking that if the world by some impossible chance really was as she made it out to be, then she was bound to try and get in touch to tell me that I was wrong and she was right—that there was a God, eternal life, a place where consciousness went. All that guff. And that she would do it somehow through a girl who looked like her. And one day one of these girls would come to me with a message.'

'And now?'

'Now it's a habit. I look at a girl and judge her by how much June there is in her. Those girls who passed us just now . . .'

'Yes?'

'The one on the left. Didn't you see? She's got June's mouth and something of her cheekbones.'

'I didn't see her face.'

Bernard tightened his grip on my arm. 'I have to ask you this because it's on my mind. I've been wanting to ask for a long time. Did she talk in a very personal way—about me and her?'

The awkward memory of the 'size' Bernard 'took' made me fumble. 'Of course. You were very much on her mind.'

'But what kind of thing?'

By withholding one set of embarrassing details, I felt I owed another. 'Well, er, she told me about the first time you . . . about your first time.'

'Ah.' Bernard withdrew his hand and put it in his pocket. We walked in silence while he considered this. Ahead we could see that parked in a ragged file down the middle of June 17 was an array of media vehicles, mobile control rooms, satellite dishes, hoisting cranes, and generator trucks. Under the trees of the Tiergarten, German workmen were unloading a matching set of dark green portable lavatories. Little muscles flinched along the line of Bernard's enormous jaw. His voice was distant. He was about to become angry.

'And this is the sort of thing you're going to be writing about?'

'Well, I haven't even begun to—'

'Does it occur to you to consider my feelings in this?'

'I was always going to show you whatever I wrote. You know that.'

'For God's sake! What was she thinking of, telling you that sort of thing?'

We had drawn level with the first of the satellite dishes. From out of the darkness empty Styrofoam coffee cups rolled toward us, propelled by a breeze. Bernard crunched one underfoot. From the crowd gathered before the Gate, still over a hundred yards ahead, there came a round of clapping. It was of the foolish, well-meaning kind you might hear from a concert audience when the grand piano is lifted onto the stage.

'Listen, Bernard, what she told me was no more intimate than your story of your row at the station. If you want to know, its main feature was what a bold step it was for a young girl in those days, proving just how attracted to you she was. And in fact, you came out of it rather well. It seemed you were, well, extremely good at that sort of thing—*genius* was the word she used. She told me how you leaped across the room and opened a window during a storm and made Tarzan noises and thousands of leaves blew in—'

Bernard had to shout above the roar of a diesel generator. 'Good Lord! That wasn't then! That was two years later. That was in Italy, when we were living above old man Massimo and his scraggy wife. They wouldn't have any noise in the house. We used to do it outside, in the fields, anywhere we could find. Then one night there's this tremendous storm blowing up, forced us indoors, so noisy they didn't hear us anyway.'

'Well—' I started to say. Bernard's anger had removed itself to June.

'What was she doing, making that up? Cooking the books, that's what! Our first time was a disaster, a complete bloody disaster. She's rewritten it for the official version. It's the airbrush all over again.'

'If you want to put the record straight . . .'

Bernard gave me a quick look of focused contempt and moved further away as he said, 'It isn't my idea of a memoir, writing up someone's sex life as if it were a damned spectator event. Is this what you think life comes down to in the end? Banging away? Sexual triumphs and failures? All good for a laugh?'

We were passing a television truck. I had a glimpse inside of a dozen or so monitors, each showing the same image of a reporter frowning at the notes in one hand while in the other an absently held microphone dangled over its loop of cable. From the crowd came a loud sigh, a long surging moan of disapproval, which began to gather in volume to a roar.

Bernard had a sudden change of mind. He swung round

to me. 'By God, you're so keen to know,' he cried. 'I'll tell you this. My wife might have been interested in poetic truth, or spiritual truth, or her own private truth, but she didn't give a damn for *truth,* for the facts, for the kind of truth that two people could recognize independently of each other. She made patterns, she invented myths. Then she made the facts fit them. For God's sake, forget about sex. Here's your subject —how people like June bend the facts to fit their ideas instead of the other way round. Why do people do that? Why do they go on doing it?'

I was hesitating over the obvious rejoinder as we came up to the edges of the crowd. Two or three thousand had gathered in the hope of seeing the Wall come down at its most important symbolic point. On the twelve-foot-high concrete blocks that straddled the approach to the Gate, a line of nervous young East German soldiers were standing at ease, facing west. They were wearing their service revolvers tucked away out of sight in the small of their backs. An officer walked up and down in front of the line, smoking and watching the crowd. Behind the soldiers rose the illuminated flaking façade of the Brandenburg Gate, with the flag of the German Democratic Republic just stirring. Barriers held the crowd back, and the moans of disappointment must have been for the West Berlin police, who were positioning their vans in front of the concrete blocks. As we arrived, someone tossed a full beer can at one of the soldiers. It flew high and fast, trailing white foam picked out by the overhead lights, and as it passed over the young soldier's head there were immediate shouts of disapproval from the crowd and calls in German for no violence. The spread of sound made me realize that there were dozens of people up in the trees.

It was not difficult to push our way to the front. Now we were among it, the crowd was more civilized, more varied than I had thought. Small children sat on their parents' shoulders, with a view as good as Bernard's. Two students were selling balloons and ice cream. A old man with dark glasses and a white cane stood still with his head cocked, listening. A wide space had been left around him. When we arrived at the barrier, Bernard pointed to where a West Berlin police officer was in conversation with an East German army officer. 'Discussing crowd control. Halfway to unification already.'

Since his outburst, Bernard had become detached in his manner. He stared around him with a cool, imperious look that was hard to reconcile with his excitement early that morning. It was as though these people and the event had a certain fascination, but only up to a point.

After half an hour it was obvious that nothing was going to happen to satisfy the crowd. There were no cranes in sight to lift away sections of the Wall, no heavy machinery to push aside the concrete blocks. But Bernard was for staying. So we stood about in the cold. A crowd is a slow, stupid creature, far less intelligent than any one of its members. This one was prepared to stand all night, with the patience of a dog, waiting for what we all knew could not happen. I began to feel irritable. Elsewhere in the city were joyful celebrations; here there was only dull patience and Bernard's senatorial calm. Another hour went by before I was able to persuade him to walk with me toward Checkpoint Charlie.

We were on a muddy path close by the Wall, whose lurid graffiti were rendered monochromatic by streetlight. On our right were abandoned buildings, empty sites with coils of wire and heaped rubble and last summer's weeds still standing high. I was no longer inclined to suppress my question.

'But you stayed in the party ten years. You must have bent an awful lot of facts yourself to manage that.'

I wanted to stir him out of his self-satisfied calm. But he shrugged his high shoulders and hunched deeper into his coat and said, 'Of course.'

He paused for a noisy band of American students to squeeze by us in a narrow passage between the Wall and a derelict building. 'What are those lines of Isaiah Berlin's that everybody quotes, especially these days, about the fatal quality of utopias? He says, If I know for certain how to bring humanity to peace, justice, happiness, boundless creativity, what price can be too high? To make this omelette, there can be no limit on the eggs I might need to break. Knowing what I know, I wouldn't be doing my duty if I couldn't accept that thousands may have to die now so that millions can be happy forever. Hardly how we put it to ourselves at the time, but it's right about the frame of mind. If you ignored or reshaped a few uncomfortable facts for the cause of party unity, what was that to the torrent of lies from what we used to call the capitalist propaganda machine? So you press on with the good work, and all the time the tide is moving up around you. June and I were latecomers, so we had the water round our ankles from the start. The news we didn't want to hear was trickling through. The show trials and purges of the thirties, enforced collectivization, mass transportations, labor camps, censorship, lies, persecution, genocide. . . . Finally the contradictions are too much for you and you crack. But you always do it later than you should. I went in 'fifty-six, I almost went in 'fifty-three, and I should have gone in 'forty-eight. But you hang on. You think, The ideas are good but the wrong people are in charge and that will change. And how can you let all this good work go to waste? You tell yourself that it was always bound to be difficult and the practice hasn't quite squared up to the theory yet and it all takes time. You tell yourself that most of what you're hearing is Cold War smears. And how can you be so wrong, how can so many intelligent, brave, good-willed people be wrong?

'If I hadn't had a scientific training, I think I might have hung on even longer. Laboratory work teaches you better than anything how easy it is to bend a result to fit a theory. It isn't even a matter of dishonesty. It's in our nature—our desires permeate our perceptions. A well-designed experiment guards against it, but this one had long been out of control. The fantasy and the reality were pulling me apart. Hungary was the last thing. I cracked.'

He paused before saying with deliberation, 'And that's the difference between June and me. She left the party years before me, but she never cracked, she never sorted the fantasy from the reality. She swapped one utopia for another. Politico or priestess, it didn't matter, in essence she was a hardliner.'

This was how it came about that I was the one who lost his temper. We were passing by that section of wasteland and Wall still known as Potsdamerplatz, threading our way through clusters of friends gathered around the steps of the viewing platform and souvenir kiosk, waiting for something to happen. What struck me then was not simply the injustice of Bernard's remarks, but a wild impatience at the difficulty of communication, and an image of parallel mirrors in place of lovers on a bed, throwing back in infinite regression likenesses paling into untruth. As I turned on Bernard, my wrist knocked something soft and warm from the hand of a man standing near me. It was a hot dog. But I was too agitated to apologize. People at Potsdamerplatz were starved for interest; heads turned our way as I shouted, and a circle began to form around us.

'That's crap, Bernard! It's worse, it's malicious! You're a liar!'

'Dear boy.'

'You never listened to what she was telling you. She wouldn't listen either. You accused each other of the same thing. She was no more of a hardliner than you are. Two softies! You loaded each other with your own guilt.'

Behind me I heard my last words being translated in a low rapid murmur into German. Bernard was trying to usher me out of the circle. But I was elated in my anger and I would not move.

'She told me she'd always loved you. You've said the same. How could you waste so much time, and everyone else's time, and your children . . . ?'

It was this last incomplete accusation that touched Bernard beyond embarrassment. His mouth tightened in a line and he stepped away from me. Suddenly my anger was gone, and in its place was the inevitable remorse; who was this upstart, presuming to describe at shouting pitch a marriage as old as himself, right into the face of the distinguished gentleman? The crowd had lost interest and was drifting back to the queue for scale-model watchtowers and postcards of no-man's-land and the empty beaches of the death strip.

We were walking on. I was in too much turmoil to apologize. My only retraction was a lowered voice and a pretense at reasonableness. We walked side by side, quicker than before. Bernard's own flurry of feeling was evident in the expressionless set of his face.

I said, 'She didn't go from one fantasy utopia to another. It was a search. She didn't claim to have all the answers. It was a quest, one she would have liked everyone to be on in their own way, but she wasn't forcing anyone. How could she? She wasn't mounting an inquisition. She had no interest in dogma or organized religion. It was a spiritual journey. Isaiah Berlin's description doesn't apply. There was no final end for which she would have sacrificed others. There were no eggs to break.'

The prospect of debate revived Bernard. He pounced, and at once I felt forgiven. 'You're wrong, dear boy, quite wrong. Calling what she was on a quest doesn't alter the fact of her absolutist streak. You were either with her, doing what she was doing, or you were out. She wanted to meditate and study mystical texts, that sort of thing, and that was fine, but it wasn't for me. I preferred to join the Labour party. She wouldn't have that. In the end she insisted on us living apart. I was one of the eggs. The children were among the others.'

While Bernard was speaking I was wondering what I was about, attempting to reconcile him to a dead wife.

So when he finished, I signaled acceptance with my open hands and said, 'Well, what did you miss in her when she died?'

We had come to one of those places along the Wall where cartography and some long-forgotten political obduracy had forced a sudden kink, a change in direction of the sector boundary, which reverted after only a few yards. Right by it was a deserted viewing platform. Without a word, Bernard began to climb the steps, and I followed. At the top he pointed.

'Look.'

Sure enough, the watchtower across from us was already deserted, and below, in the glare of fluorescent lights, moving peaceably over the raked sand that concealed land mines, booby traps, and automatic guns, were dozens of rabbits, searching out fringes of grass to nibble.

'Well, something flourished.'

'Their time is almost up.'

We stood in silence for a while. Our view was back along the direction of the Wall, which was in fact two walls, at this point a hundred and fifty yards apart. I had never visited the border at night, and staring down this broad corridor of wire, sand, service road, and symmetrical lampheads, I was struck by the innocent brightness, the shameless indignity; where traditionally states kept their atrocities well hidden, here the advertisement was more lurid than any Kurfürstendamm neon.

'Utopia.'

Bernard sighed, and might have been about to reply when we heard voices and laughter from different directions. Then the observation stand began to tremble as people came stomping up the wooden steps. Our isolation had been mere chance, a hole in the crowd. Within seconds fifteen others were squeezed up around us, clicking cameras and calling excitedly in German, Japanese, and Danish. We pushed our way down against the flow and continued on our way.

I assumed Bernard had forgotten my question, or preferred not to answer it, but as we came to where our path ran alongside the steps of the old Reichstag building, he said,

'What I miss most is her seriousness. She was one of the few people I know who saw her life as a project, an undertaking, something to take control of and direct toward—well, understanding, wisdom, on her own particular terms. Most of us reserve our forward planning for money, careers, children, that sort of thing. June wanted to understand, God knows, herself, existence, "creation." She was very impatient with the rest of us, drifting through, taking one thing after another, "sleepwalking," she called it. I hated the nonsense she filled her head with, but I loved her seriousness.'

We had come to the edge of a large hole, a sixty-foot-long trench at basement level, on a site of earth heaps. Bernard stopped here and added, 'Over the years we either fought or we ignored each other, but you're right, she did love me, and when that's taken from you . . .' He gestured toward the hole. 'I've been reading about this. It's the old Gestapo headquarters. They're digging it up, researching the past. I don't know how anyone of my generation could accept that—Gestapo crimes neutralized by archaeology.'

I saw now that the trench had been dug along the line of what once must have been an access corridor to the series of white-tiled cells we were looking down into. Each one was barely big enough for one prisoner, and in each there were two iron rings set into the wall. On the far side of the site was a low building, the museum.

Bernard said, 'They'll find a fingernail extracted from some poor wretch, clean it up, and shove it in a glass case with a label. And half a mile over there, the Stasi will be cleaning out their cells too.' The bitterness in his voice surprised me, and I turned to look at him. He leaned his weight against an iron post. He looked weary, and thinner than ever, hardly more than a post himself inside his overcoat. He had been on his feet for almost three hours, and now he was drained further by residual anger from a war only the old and weak could remember at first hand.

'You need a rest,' I said. 'There's a café just up here, by Checkpoint Charlie.'

I had no idea how far it was. As I led him away, I noticed how stiff and slow his steps were. I blamed myself for my thoughtlessness. We were crossing a road chopped to a cul-de-sac by the Wall. Bernard's face by streetlight was a sweaty gray, and his eyes looked too bright. His big jaw, that friendliest aspect of his huge face, showed a faint tremor of senility. I was caught between the need to hurry him along toward warmth and food and the fear that he might collapse altogether. I had no idea how one summoned an ambulance in West Berlin, and here in the derelict fringes of the border there were no phones and even the Germans were tourists. I asked him if he wanted to sit and rest a while, but he did not seem to hear me.

I was repeating my question when I heard a car horn and a ragged cheer. The concentrated illumination of Checkpoint Charlie projected a milky halo from behind a deserted building ahead of us. Within minutes we emerged, right by the café, and before us was the dreamlike slow-motion familiarity of the scene I had watched with Jenny that morning: the frontier furniture of guardrooms, multilingual signs, and stripy gates, and the well-wishers still greeting pedestrians from the east, still thumping Trabant rooftops, but with less passion now, as though to demonstrate a difference between TV drama and real life.

I had hold of Bernard's arm as we paused to take this in. Then we edged through the crowd toward the café's entrance. But the people we passed were in a queue. They were being let inside only as spaces became vacant. Who would want to give up a table at this hour of the night? Through windows mottled by condensation we could see the privileged eaters and drinkers wrapped in their fug.

I was about to force a way in, pleading medical necessity, when Bernard broke free and hurried away from me to cross the road toward the traffic island where most of the crowd was standing, by the American guardroom. Until then I hadn't seen what he had seen. Later he assured me that all the elements of the situation had been in place when we arrived, but it was only when I called after him and followed him that I saw the red flag. It was supported on a short pole, a sawed-off broomstick perhaps, held by a slight man in his early twenties. He looked Turkish. He had black curls and black clothes—a black double-breasted jacket worn over a black T-shirt and black jeans. He was strolling up and down in front of the crowd, head tipped back, the flag on its pole slanted across his shoulder. When he stepped backward into the path of a Wartburg he refused to move, and the car was obliged to maneuver around him.

As a provocation it was already beginning to succeed, and this was what was drawing Bernard toward the road. The young man's antagonists were a mixed bunch, but what I saw in that first instant were two men in suits—business types or solicitors—right by the curb. As the young man passed, one of them flicked him under the chin. It was not so much a blow as an expression of contempt. The romantic revolutionary jerked away and pretended nothing had happened. An old lady in a fur hat screamed a long sentence at him and raised an umbrella. She was restrained by the gentleman at her side. The flag man raised his standard higher. The second solicitor type took a step forward and punched out at his ear. It did not connect well, but it was enough to make the young man falter. Disdaining to touch the side of his head where the punch had landed, he continued his parade. By this time Bernard was halfway across the road and I was just behind.

As far as I was concerned, the flag man could have what he was asking for. My anxiety was for Bernard. His left knee seemed to be giving him trouble, but he was limping ahead of me at a fair pace. He had already seen what was coming next, an uglier manifestation, coming at a run from the direction of Koch Strasse. There were half a dozen of them, calling to one another as they came. I heard the words they were calling, but at the time I ignored them. I preferred to think that a long evening in the rejoicing city had starved them of action. They had seen a man punched in the head and had been energized. They were aged between sixteen and twenty. Collectively they exuded a runtish viciousness, an extravagant air of underprivilege, with their acned pallor, shaved heads, and loose wet mouths. The Turk saw them charging toward him and tossed his head like a tango dancer and turned his back. To be out here doing this on the day of communism's final disgrace showed either a martyr's zeal or an unfathomable masochistic urge to be beaten up in public. It was true that most of the crowd would have dismissed him as a crank and ignored him. Berlin was a tolerant place, after all. But tonight there was just sufficient drunkenness, and a vague sense in a few people that someone ought to be blamed for something—and the man with the flag seemed to have found them all in one place.

I drew level with Bernard and put my hand on his arm. 'Stay out of this, Bernard. You could get hurt.'

'Nonsense,' he said, and shook his arm free.

We arrived at the young man's side several seconds before the kids. He smelled strongly of patchouli, which was not, to my mind, the true scent of Marxist-Leninist thought. Surely he was a fraud. I just had time to say, 'Come on!' and I was still tugging at Bernard's arm when the gang arrived. He stood between the boys and their victim and spread his arms.

'Now then,' he said, in the old-fashioned kindly-stern voice of an English bobby. Did he really think he was too old, too tall and thin, too eminent to be hit? The kids had stopped short and were bunched up in a pack, breathing heavily, heads and tongues lolling in bemusement at this beanpole, this scarecrow in a coat who stood in their way. I saw that two of them had silver swastikas pinned to their lapels. Another had a swastika tattoo on his knuckle. I did not dare turn around to look, but I had the impression that the Turk was taking the opportunity to roll up his flag and slip away. The solicitor types, amazed by what their own violence had conjured up, had retreated deeper into the crowd to watch.

I looked around for help. An American sergeant and two soldiers had their backs to us as they walked to confer with their East German counterparts. Among the kids the bemusement was turning to anger. Suddenly two of them ran around

Bernard, but the flag man had already forced a way through to the back of the crowd, and now he was sprinting up the road. He turned the corner into Koch Strasse and was gone.

The two gave halfhearted pursuit and then came back to us. Bernard would have to do instead.

'Now off you go,' he said brightly, shooing them with the backs of his hands. I was wondering whether it was more understandable or rather more loathsome that these people with swastikas should be German, when the smallest of them, a pin-headed tyke in a bomber jacket, nipped forward and kicked Bernard on the shin. I heard the thud of boot on bone. With a little sigh of surprise, Bernard folded up in sections onto the pavement.

There was a groan of disapproval from the crowd, but nobody moved. I stepped forward and swung out at the boy and missed. But he and his friends were not interested in me. They were gathering around Bernard, ready, I thought, to kick him to death. One last glance toward the guardroom showed no sign of the sergeant or the soldiers. I jerked one of the boys back by his collar and was trying to reach for another. There were too many for me. I saw two, perhaps three black boots withdrawing on the backswing.

But they did not move. They froze in place, for just then, out of the crowd there sprang a figure who whirled about us, lashing the boys with staccato sentences of piercing rebuke. It was a furious young woman. Her power was of the street. She had credibility. She was a contemporary, an object of desire and aspiration. She was a star, and she had caught them being vile, even by their own standards.

The force of her disgust was sexual. They thought they were men, and she was reducing them to naughty children.

They could not afford to be seen shrinking from her, backing off. But that was exactly what they were doing now, even though the outward signs were laughs, shrugs, and the unheard insults they called out to her. They pretended to themselves, to one another, that they were suddenly bored, that it would be more interesting elsewhere. They began moving back toward Koch Strasse, but the woman did not let up her tirade. They probably would have liked to run from her, but protocol obliged them to keep to a forced, self-conscious swagger. While she followed them down the street, shouting and waving her fist, they had to keep the catcalls coming and their thumbs hooked in their jeans.

I was helping Bernard to his feet. It was only when the young woman came back to see how he was, and her identically dressed friend appeared at her side, that I recognized them as the two who had swished past us on June 17th Street. Together we supported Bernard while he tested his weight on his leg. It did not appear to be broken. There was some applause in the crowd for him as he put his arm around my shoulder and we shuffled away from the Checkpoint.

It took us several minutes to reach the corner of the street where we hoped to find a taxi. During that time I was anxious to have Bernard acknowledge the identity of his rescuer. I asked her her name—Grete—and repeated it to him. He was concentrating on his pain, he was bent over it, and he may have been in mild shock, but I persisted in the interest of —what, exactly? Unsettling the rationalist? In him? In me?

Finally Bernard lifted a hand in the girl's direction for her to take and said, 'Grete, thank you, my dear. You saved my bacon.' But he was not looking at her as he said it.

On Koch Strasse I thought I would have time to ask

Grete and her friend, Diane, about themselves, but as soon as we arrived we saw a taxi dropping people off and we called it over. There followed the hiatus of easing Bernard in, and thanks and farewells and thanks again, during which I hoped he would at last take a look at his guardian angel, the incarnation of June. I waved to the girls out of the rear window as they walked away, and before giving the driver his instructions, I said to Bernard, 'Didn't you recognize them? They were the ones we saw by the Brandenburg Gate, when you told me how you used to expect a message from—'

Bernard was arranging his head, tipping it right back against the head rest, and he interrupted me with a sigh. He spoke impatiently to the padded ceiling of the car, inches from his nose. 'Yes. Quite a coincidence, I suppose. Now for goodness' sake Jeremy, get me home!'

3

· · · · · · · · · · · · · ·

Majdanek
Les Salces
St. Maurice
de Navacelles,
1989

The following day he did not stir from the apartment in Kreuzberg. He lay on a couch in the tiny living room looking morose, preferring the television to conversation. A doctor friend of Gunter's called round to examine the injured leg. It was likely that nothing was broken, but an X ray in London was recommended. I went out for a stroll in the late morning. The streets had a hungover look, with beer cans and smashed bottles underfoot and, around the hot dog stalls, paper napkins smeared with mustard and tomato ketchup. During the afternoon, while Bernard slept, I read the newspapers and wrote up our conversations of the day before. In the evening he was still untalkative. I went out for another stroll and had a beer in a local *Kneipe*. The festivities were beginning again, but I had seen enough. I was back in the apartment within an hour, and we were both asleep by half past ten.

Bernard's flight the next morning to London and mine to Montpellier via Frankfurt and Paris were only an hour apart. I had arranged for one of Jenny's brothers to meet the plane at Heathrow. Bernard was livelier. He hobbled across the terminal at Tegel looking well suited to the walking stick he had borrowed, using it to hail an airline employee and remind him of the wheelchair that had been ordered. It would be waiting, Bernard was assured, by the departure gate.

As we walked in that direction I said, 'Bernard, I wanted to ask you something about June's dogs—'

He interrupted me. 'For the life and times? I'll tell you something. You can forget all that nonsense about "face to face with evil." Religious cant. But you know, I was the one who told her about Churchill's black dog. You remember? The name he gave to the depressions he used to get from time to time. I think he pinched the expression from Samuel Johnson. So June's idea was that if one dog was a personal depression, two dogs were a kind of cultural depression, civilization's worst moods. Not bad, really. I've often made use of it. It went through my mind at Checkpoint Charlie. It wasn't his red flag, you know. I don't think they even saw it. You heard what they were shouting?'

'*Ausländer 'raus.*'

'Foreigners out. The Wall comes down and everybody's out there dancing in the street, but sooner or later . . .'

We had arrived at the departure gate. A man in a

braided uniform maneuvered the wheelchair behind Bernard, and he lowered himself with a sigh.

I said, 'But that wasn't my question. I was looking at my old notes yesterday. The last time I saw June, she told me to ask you what the *Maire* of St. Maurice de Navacelles said about those dogs when you had lunch at the café that afternoon.'

'The Hôtel des Tilleuls? What those dogs had been trained to do? A perfect case in point. The *Maire*'s story simply wasn't true. Or at the very least, there was no way of knowing. But June chose to believe it because it fitted nicely. A perfect case of bending the facts to the idea.'

I handed Bernard's bags to the flight attendant, who stowed it behind the wheelchair. Then he stood with his hands in the pushing position, waiting for us to finish. Bernard leaned back with his stick across his lap. It bothered me that my father-in-law should take so easily to his invalid status.

'But Bernard,' I said. 'What was the story? What did he say those dogs had been trained to do?'

Bernard shook his head. 'Another time. Dear boy, thank you for coming along.' Then he raised his rubber-tipped stick, partly in salute, partly as a signal to the attendant, who nodded to me curtly and wheeled his passenger away.

I was too restless to make good use of my hour's wait. I lingered by a bar wondering if I needed one last coffee, one final German thing to eat. At the bookshop I browsed at length without buying even a paper, having glutted on them for three hours the day before. I still had twenty minutes, time enough for another slow wander around the terminal. Often when I am in transit in a foreign airport and not bound for England, I glance up at the departure board, at the London flights, to gauge in myself the tidal pull of home, Jenny, family. What came now as I noted only one flight announced—on the international flight map, Berlin was a backwater—was one of my earliest memories of my wife, prompted by something Bernard had just said.

In October 1981 I was in Poland as a member of an amorphous cultural delegation invited by the Polish government. I was then the administrator of a moderately successful provincial theater company. Among the group were a novelist, an arts journalist, a translator, and two or three culture bureaucrats. The only woman was Jenny Tremaine, who represented an institution based in Paris and funded from Brussels. Because she was both beautiful and rather brisk in her manner, she drew hostility from some of the men. The novelist in particular, aroused by the paradox of an attractive woman unimpressed by his reputation, had a racing bet with the journalist and one of the bureaucrats to see who could 'pull' her first. The general idea was that Miss Tremaine, with her white freckled skin and green eyes, her head of thick red hair, her efficient way with her appointment book and perfect French, had to be put in her place. In the inevitable boredom of an official visit there was a good deal of muttering over late-night drinks in the hotel bar. The effect was souring. It was impossible to exchange a word or two with this woman, whose sharp style, I soon discovered, merely concealed her nervousness, without some of the others nudging and winking in the background, and asking me later if I was 'in the race.'

What made me angrier was that in a sense, only in a sense, I was. Within days of our arrival in Warsaw I was stricken, lovesick, an old-fashioned hopeless case, and for the gleeful novelist and his friends, a hilarious complication. The first sight of her each day at breakfast as she made her way across the hotel restaurant toward our table caused in me such a painful tightness in the chest, such a hollow, falling sensation in my stomach, that when she arrived I could neither ignore her nor be casually polite without revealing myself to the others. My hard-boiled egg and black bread remained untouched.

There were no opportunities to talk to her alone. All day long we sat in committee rooms or lecture theaters with editors, translators, journalists, government officials, and Solidarity people, for this was the time of Solidarity's ascendancy, and though we could not know it, only weeks from its end, its banishment after General Jaruzelski's coup. There was only one conversation: Poland. Its urgency swirled around us and pressed in as we moved from one dim, grubby room, one cigarette haze, to another. What was Poland? What was Solidarity? Could democracy flourish? Would it survive? Would the Russians invade? Did Poland belong in Europe? What about the peasants? Food lines were growing longer by the day. The government blamed Solidarity, everyone else blamed the government. There were marches in the street, baton charges by the Zomo police, a student occupation at the university, and more all-night discussions. I had never given Poland much thought before, but inside a week I became, like everyone else, foreigners and Poles alike, a passionate expert, if not in the answers, then in the right kind of questions. My own politics were thrown into turmoil. Poles whom I instinctively admired urged me to support the very Western politicians I most distrusted, and a language of anticommunism—which until then I had associated with cranky ideologues of the right—came easily to everyone here, where communism was a network of privileges and corruption and licensed violence, a mental disease, an array of laughable, improbable lies, and, most tangibly, the instrument of occupation by a foreign power.

At every venue, somewhere, several chairs away, was Jenny Tremaine. My throat ached, my eyes stung from cigarettes in unventilated rooms, I was dizzy and sick from late nights and daily hangovers, I had a heavy cold and could never find tissues to blow my nose on, and I ran a constant high temperature. On my way to attend a session on Polish theater I was sick in the gutter, to the disgust of the women in a nearby breadline, who thought I was a drunk. My fever, elation, and affliction were, inextricably, Poland, Jenny, and the gloating, cynical novelist and his sidekicks, whom I had come to despise and who loved to count me in their number and provoke me by disclosing where, according to them, I stood that day in the running.

At the beginning of our second week Jenny astounded me by asking me to accompany her to the town of Lublin, one hundred miles away. She wanted to visit the concentration camp of Majdanek in order to take photographs for a friend who was writing a book. Three years before, in a previous job as a television researcher, I had been to Belsen and had promised myself that I would never look at another camp. One visit was a necessary education; a second was morbid. But now this ghostly pale woman was inviting me to return. At the time we were standing outside my room, just after breakfast. We were already late for the first appointment of the day, and she seemed to want an immediate answer. She explained that she had never visited a concentration camp before and preferred to go with someone she could think of as a friend. As she arrived at this last word she brushed the back of my hand with her fingers. Her touch was cool. I took her hand and then, because she had taken a willing step toward me, I kissed her. It was a long kiss in the gloomy, unpeopled emptiness of the hotel corridor. At the sound of a door handle turning we stopped, and I told her that I would gladly go with her. Then someone was calling me from the stairs. There was no time to speak again until the following morning, when we arranged to travel by taxi.

In those days the Polish zloty was at its most abject, and the American dollar was supreme. It was possible to hire a car to take us to Lublin, wait for us there overnight if necessary, then drive us back, all for twenty dollars. We managed to slip away without being observed by the novelist and his friends. The kiss, the feel of it, the extraordinary fact of it, the expectation of another and of what lay beyond, had preoccupied me for twenty-four hours. But now, as we headed out through the drab outskirts of Warsaw, conscious of our destination, this kiss receded before us. We sat well apart on the back seat of the Lada and exchanged basic information about our lives. This was when I learned that she was the daughter of Bernard Tremaine, whose name I vaguely knew from radio programs and his biography of Nasser. Jenny talked about her parents' estrangement and her difficult relations with her mother, who lived alone in a remote place in France and who had abandoned the world in pursuit of a life of spiritual meditation. At this first reference to June I was already curious to meet her. I told Jenny about my parents' death in a car accident when I was eight, and growing up with my sister, Jean, and my niece, Sally, to whom I was still a kind of father, and how adept I was at moving in on other people's parents. I think that even then we joked about how I might insinuate myself into the affections of Jenny's prickly mother.

My unreliable memory of the Poland that lay between Warsaw and Lublin is of one immense brownish black ploughed field traversed by a straight treeless road. It was snowing lightly when we arrived. We took the advice of Polish friends and asked to be dropped in the center of Lublin and set out from there. I had not fully understood how close the town was to the camp that had consumed all its Jews, three quarters of its population. They lay side by side, Lublin and Majdanek, matter and antimatter. We stopped outside the main entrance to read a sign that announced that so many hundreds of thousands of Poles, Lithuanians, Russians, French, British, and Americans had died here. It was very quiet. There was no one in sight. I felt a momentary reluctance to enter. Jenny's whisper startled me.

'No mention of the Jews. See? It still goes on. And it's official.' Then she added, more to herself, 'The black dogs.'

These last words I ignored. As for the rest, even discounting the hyperbole, a residual truth was sufficient to transform Majdanek for me in an instant from a monument, an honorable civic defiance of oblivion, to a disease of the imagination and a living peril, a barely conscious connivance with evil. I linked my arm through Jenny's and we went on in, past the outer fences, past the guardroom, which was still in use. On its doorstep stood two full bottles of milk. An inch of snow was the latest addition to the camp's obsessive neatness. We walked across a no-man's-land, and let our arms drop to our sides. Ahead were the watchtowers, squat huts on stilts with steeply pitched roofs and shaky wooden ladders; they commanded a view between the double inner fence. Contained by this were the huts, longer, lower, and more numerous than I had imagined. They filled our horizon. Beyond them, floating free against the orange-white sky, like a dirty tramp steamer with a single stack, was the incinerator. We did not speak for an hour. Jenny read her instructions and took the photographs. We followed a party of schoolchildren into a hut where wire cages were crammed full of shoes, tens of thousands of them, flattened and curled like dried fruit. In another hut, more shoes, and in a third, unbelievably, more, no longer caged but spilling in their thousands across the floor. I saw a hobnail boot beside a baby shoe whose nursery lamb still showed through the dust. Life turned to tat. The extravagant numerical scale, the easy-to-say numbers—tens and hundreds of thousands, millions—denied the imagination its proper sympathies, its rightful grasp of the suffering, and one was drawn insidiously to the persecutors' premise, that life was cheap, junk to be inspected in heaps. As we walked on, my emotions died. There was nothing we could do to help. There was no one to feed or free. We were strolling like tourists. Either you came here and despaired, or you put your hands deeper into your pockets and gripped your warm loose change and found that you had taken one step closer to the dreamers of the nightmare. This was our inevitable shame, our share in the misery. We were on the other side, we walked here freely like the commandant once did, or his political master, poking into this or that, knowing the way out, in the full certainty of our next meal.

After a while I could no longer bear the victims and I thought only of their persecutors. We were walking among the huts. How well they were constructed, how well they had lasted. Neat paths joined each front door to the track we were on. The huts stretched so far ahead of us, I could not see to the end of the row. And this was only one row, in one part of the camp, and this was only one camp, a small one by comparison. I sank into inverted admiration, bleak wonder; to dream of this enterprise, to plan these camps, to build them and take such pains, to furnish, run, and maintain them, and to marshal from towns and villages their human fuel—such energy, such dedication. How could one begin to call it a mistake?

We met up with the children again and followed them into the brick building with a chimney. Like everyone else, we noted the maker's name on the oven doors. A special order promptly filled. We saw an old container of hydrogen cyanide, Zyklon B, supplied by the firm of Degesch. On our way out, Jenny spoke for the first time in an hour to tell me that in one day in November 1943 the German authorities had machine-gunned thirty-six thousand Jews from Lublin. They made them lie in gigantic graves and slaughtered them to the sound of amplified dance music. We talked again of the sign outside the main gate, and its omission.

'The Germans did their work for them. Even when there are no Jews left, they still hate them,' Jenny said.

Suddenly I remembered. 'What was it you said about dogs?'

'Black dogs. It's a family phrase, from my mother.' She was about to explain more, then she changed her mind.

We left the camp and we walked back into Lublin. I saw for the first time that it was an attractive town. It had escaped the destruction and postwar building that disfigured Warsaw.

We were on a steep street of wet cobbles, which a brilliant orange winter sunset had transformed into knobs of gold. It was as though we had been released from long captivity and were excited to be part of the world again, of the ordinariness of Lublin's unemphatic rush hour. Quite unselfconsciously, Jenny held my arm, and swung her camera loosely on its strap as she told me a story about a Polish friend who went to Paris to study cooking. I have already said that in matters of sex and love I was always reticent, and that it was my sister who had the easy way with seduction. But on this day, liberated from the usual constraints of selfhood, I did something uncharacteristically brilliant. I stopped Jenny mid-sentence and kissed her, and then I told her simply that she was the most beautiful woman I had ever met and that there was really nothing I wanted more than to spend the rest of the day making love to her. Her green eyes studied mine, then she raised her arm, and I thought for a moment she was about to slap my face. But she pointed across the street at a narrow door above which hung a faded sign. We trod on gold nuggets to get to the Hotel Wisła. We spent three days there, having dismissed the driver. Ten months later, we were married.

I stopped outside the dark house in the car I had rented at Montpellier airport. Then I got out and stood a while in the orchard looking at the starry November sky, overcoming my reluctance to go in. It was never a pleasant experience to return to the *bergerie* when it had been closed down for months, or even weeks. No one had been here since the end of our long summer holiday, since our noisy, chaotic depar-

ture one morning in early September, after which the last
echoes of children's voices had faded into the silence of old
stones and the *bergerie* had settled again into its longer per-
spective, not of holiday weeks or children's growing years or
even the decades of ownership, but of centuries, rural centuries. I did not really believe this, but I could imagine how, in
our absence, June's spirit, her many ghosts, might stealthily
reassert possession, recapturing not just her furniture and
kitchenware and pictures but the curl of a magazine cover,
the ancient Australia-shaped stain on the bathroom wall, and
the latent body shape of her old gardening jacket, still hanging behind a door because no one could bear to throw it out.
After an absence, the very space between objects was altered,
tilted, washed a pale brown, or the essence of that color, and
sounds—the first turning of the key in the lock—acquired a
subtly transformed acoustic, a dead echo just beyond the au-
ral range that suggested an invisible, almost answering presence. Jenny hated opening up the house. It was more difficult
at night; the place had expanded piecemeal over forty years,
and the front door was nowhere near the electricity switchboard. You had to walk right through the living room and
kitchen to reach it, and I had forgotten to bring a torch.

I opened the front door and stood before a wall of darkness. Then I reached inside, up to a shelf where we tried to
remember to keep a candle and a box of matches. There was
nothing there. I stood and listened. Whatever sensible thing I
told myself, I could not banish the thought that in a house
where a woman had given herself for so many years to the
contemplation of eternity, some delicate emanation, a gossa-
mer web of consciousness, inhered and was aware of me. I
could not bring myself to say June's name aloud, but it was

what I wanted to do, not to summon up the spirit but to chase it away. Instead I cleared my throat noisily, a skeptical, masculine sound. With the lights full on, the radio going, the whitebait I had bought at a roadside stall frying in June's olive oil, the ghosts would retreat to the shadows. Daylight would help too, but it would be a couple of days, a couple of uneasy evenings, before the house was mine again. To take immediate possession of the *bergerie* you had to arrive with children. With their rediscovery of forgotten games and projects, their laughter and the squabbling over bunk beds, the spirit gracefully conceded to the energies of the living, and you could go anywhere in the house, even into June's bedroom or her old study, without a thought.

With my hand stretched out in front of my face, I walked across the hall. Everywhere was a sweet smell I associated with June. It came from the lavender soap she had bought in bulk. We were not even halfway through her supply. I groped my way across the living room and opened the door to the kitchen. The smell here was of metal and, faintly, butane gas. The fuse box and switch were in a cupboard on the wall on the far side of the room. Even in this darkness it showed as a blacker patch ahead of me. As I edged around the kitchen table, the sensation that I was being watched intensified. The surface of my skin had become an organ of perception, sensitized to darkness and to every molecule of air. My bare arms were registering a threat. Something was up; the kitchen did not feel the same. I was moving in the wrong direction. I wanted to turn back, but that would have been ridiculous. The car was too small to sleep in. The nearest hotel was twenty-five miles away, and it was almost midnight.

The shapeless deeper black of the switchboard cupboard

was twenty feet or so away, and I was guiding myself toward it by trailing my hand along the edge of the kitchen table. Not since childhood had I been so intimidated by the dark. Like a character in a cartoon, I hummed softly, without conviction. No tune came to mind, and my random sequence of notes was foolish. My voice sounded weak. I deserved to be harmed. Once again the thought came, clearer this time, that all I needed to do was leave. My hand brushed against something hard and round. It was the knob on the end of the table's drawer. I almost pulled on it, but I decided not to. I made myself go on until I was standing free of the table. The patch on the wall was so black it throbbed. It had a center but no edges. I put my hand up toward it, and it was then that my nerve failed. I did not dare touch it. I took a step back and stood there, locked in indecision. I was trapped between my reason, which urged me to move quickly, turn on the power, and see by bright artificial light how ordinariness simply continued, as it always did, and my superstitious dread, whose simplicity was even greater than the everyday.

I must have stood for more than five minutes. At one point I almost strode forward to wrench open the switchboard door, but the first signals to my legs did not get through. I knew that if I left the kitchen, I would not be able to return to it that night. And so I stood there until at last I remembered the kitchen drawer and why I had been about to open it. The candle and the box of matches that should have been by the front door might be there. I slid my hand back along the table, found the drawer, and groped among the garden clippers and thumbtacks and string.

The stub of a candle, barely two inches long, lit at first attempt. The shadows of the switchboard cupboard bobbed against the wall at my approach. It looked different. The little wooden handle on its door was longer, more ornate, and set at a new angle. I was two feet away when the ornamentation resolved itself into the form of a scorpion, fat and yellow, its pincers curved about the axis of the diagonal and its chunkily segmented tail just obscuring the handle beneath.

These creatures are ancient chelicerates who trace their ancestry back to cambrian times, almost 600 million years ago, and it is a kind of innocence, a hopeless ignorance of modern, post-Holocene conditions, that brings them into the homes of the newfangled apes; you find them squatting on walls in exposed places, their claws and sting pathetic, outdated defenses against the obliterating swipe of a shoe. I took a heavy wooden spoon from the kitchen counter and killed this one with a single blow. It dropped to the floor, and I stamped on it for good measure. I still had to overcome a reluctance to touch the place where its body had been. I remembered now that years ago we had found a nest of baby scorpions in this same cupboard.

The lights came on; the bulbous fifties fridge shuddered and began its familiar rattling lament. I was anxious not to reflect immediately on my experience. I brought in my luggage, made up a bed, cooked the fish, played an old Art Pepper record at full volume, and drank half a bottle of wine. I had no trouble falling asleep at three in the morning. The following day I set about preparing the house for our December holiday. I worked my way through the beginning of my list, spending several hours on the roof fixing tiles dislodged in a September storm, and the rest of the day on jobs about the house. The weather was warm, and toward the late afternoon I slung the hammock in June's favorite spot, under the tamarisk tree. Lying here I had a view of golden light hanging in the valley toward St. Privat, and beyond, the winter sun low over the hills around Lodève. I had been thinking about my fright all day. Two indistinct voices had followed me around the house as I did my work, and now as I sprawled with a pot of tea at my side they grew clearer.

June was impatient. 'How can you pretend to doubt what's staring you in the face? How can you be so perverse, Jeremy? You sensed my presence as soon as you stepped into the house. You had a premonition of danger, and then confirmation that you would have been badly stung if you had ignored your feelings. I warned you, protected you, it was as simple as that, and if you're prepared to go to such lengths to keep your skepticism intact, then you're an ingrate and I should never have put myself out for you. Rationalism is a blind faith. Jeremy, how can you ever hope to see?'

Bernard was excited. 'This really is a useful illustration! Of course, you can't rule out the possibility that a form of consciousness survives death and acted here in your best interests. You should always keep an open mind. Beware of dismissing phenomena that don't accord with current theories. On the other hand, in the absence of certain proof either way, why leap straight to such a radical conclusion without considering other, simpler possibilities? You've frequently "sensed June's presence" in the house—simply another way of saying that it was once her place, is still full of her things, and that being here, especially after an absence and before your own family has filled up the rooms, is bound to prompt thoughts of her. In other words, this "presence" was in your mind, and projected by you onto the surroundings. Given our fear of the dead, it's understandable that you were wary as you stumbled through the house in darkness. And given your state of mind, the electricity cupboard on the wall was bound to seem a frightening object—a patch of extra blackness in the dark, wasn't it? You had the buried memory of finding a nest of scorpions there. And you ought to consider the possibility that in poor light you discerned the scorpion's shape subliminally. And then the fact that your presentiments were justified—well, dear boy! Scorpions are common enough in this part of France. Why shouldn't one be sitting on the cupboard? And then again, suppose it had stung you on the hand? The poison would have been easy to suck. There would have been pain and discomfort for no more than a day or two—it wasn't a black scorpion, after all. Why should a spirit from beyond the grave put itself out to save you from a minor injury? If this is the level of the dead's concern, why aren't they interceding to prevent the millions of human tragedies that happen every day?'

'Pah!' I heard June say. 'How would you know if we did? You wouldn't believe it anyway. I looked after Bernard in Berlin and you last night because I wanted to show you something, I wanted to show you how little you know about the God-made, God-filled universe. But there's no evidence a skeptic can't bend to fit his own drab, tiny scheme . . .'

'Nonsense,' Bernard murmured into my other ear. 'The world that science is revealing is a scintillating, wondrous place. We don't have to invent a god just because we don't understand it all. Our investigations have hardly begun!'

'Do you think you'd be hearing me now if some part of me did not still exist?'

'You're hearing nothing, dear boy. You're inventing us both, extrapolating from what you know. There's no one here but you.'

'There's God,' said June, 'and there's the Devil.'

'If I'm the Devil,' said Bernard, 'then the world's no bad place at all.'

'It's Bernard's innocence that's precisely the measure of his evil. You were in Berlin, Jeremy. Look at the damage he and his kind have done in the name of progress.'

'These pious monotheists! The pettiness, the intolerance, the ignorance, the cruelty they've unleashed in their certainty—'

'It's a loving God and he'll forgive Bernard—'

'We can love without a god, thank you very much. I detest the way Christians have hijacked that word.'

These voices took up residence, they pursued me and began to afflict me. The next day, when I was pruning the peach trees in the orchard, June said the tree I was working on and its beauty were God's creation. Bernard said we knew a great deal about the way this and other trees evolved and our explanations did not require a god. Statements and counterstatements chased their tails as I chopped wood, unblocked gutters, and swept out rooms. It was a drone that would not be banished. It continued even when I managed to turn my attention away. If I listened, I learned nothing. Each proposition blocked the one before or was blocked by the one that followed. It was a self-canceling argument, a multiplication of zeros, and I could not make it stop. When all my jobs were done and I spread out the notes for my memoir on the kitchen table, my in-laws raised their voices.

I tried joining in. 'Listen, you two. You're in separate

realms, you're out of each other's area of competence. It's not the business of science to prove or disprove the existence of God, and it's not the business of the spirit to measure the world.'

There was an embarrassed silence. They seemed to wait for me to go on. Then I heard Bernard, or made him, say quietly, to June, not to me, 'That's all very well. But the Church always wanted to control science. All knowledge, for that matter. Take the case of Galileo—'

And June cut across him to say, 'It was the Church that kept learning alive for centuries in Europe. Remember when we were in Cluny in 1954, that man who showed us round the library . . . ?'

When I phoned home and complained to Jenny that I thought I might be going mad, she was gleefully unconsoling.

'You wanted their stories. You encouraged them, you courted them. Now you've got them, quarrels and all.' She recovered from a second fit of laughing and asked me why I didn't write down what they were saying.

'There's no point. It just goes round and round.'

'That's just what I always said. You wouldn't listen. You're being punished for stirring it up.'

'By whom?'

'Ask my mother.'

It was another clear day when, shortly after breakfast, I abandoned all responsibilities, absolved myself of all mental tasks, and with a luxurious sense of truancy put on my walking boots, found a large-scale map, and stowed a water bottle and two oranges in my day pack.

I set off along the track that rises behind the *bergerie* and ascends northward above a dry gully, through woods of scrub oak, then winds under the massive rock of the Pas de l'Azé to reach the high plateau. At a firm pace it takes only half an hour to be up there, on the Causse de Larzac, with a cool breeze among the pines and a view toward the Pic de Vissou and beyond, forty miles away, a silvery splinter of the Mediterranean. I followed a sandy track through the pine woods, past limestone outcroppings weathered into the shapes of ruins, then onto open ground that rises toward the Bergerie de Tedenat. From there I had a view over the plateau of the few hours' walk to the village of St. Maurice de Navacelles. Less than a mile beyond it was the huge fissure of the Gorge de Vis. Somewhere to the left, on its edge, was the Dolmen de la Prunarède.

First there was the descent back through the tree line into La Vacquerie. There is a simple pleasure in entering and leaving a village on foot. Temporarily, the illusion can be sustained that while others have lives that are fixed around houses, relationships, and work, you are self-sufficient and free, unencumbered by possessions and obligations. It is a privileged sensation of lightness that cannot be had by passing through in a car, as part of the traffic. I decided against stopping at the bar for a coffee and paused only to look closely at the monument across the way and to copy into a notebook the inscription around its base.

I left the village on a minor road and turned north onto a pretty track that runs toward the gorge. For the first time since my arrival, I was truly content, and felt my old love for this deserted part of France fully restored. The nagging song of June and Bernard's quarrel was fading. So too was the restless excitement of Berlin; it was as though numerous tiny muscles in the back of my neck were slowly uncoiling, and as they did so, there opened up within me a calm, generous space to match the expansive landscape I was walking across. As I occasionally do when I am happy, I thought about the whole pattern, the thumbnail story of my existence from the age of eight until Majdanek, and how I had been delivered. A thousand miles away, in or near one house among all the millions, were Jenny and our four children, my tribe. I belonged; my life was rooted and rich. The track was even and I kept up a steady pace. I began to see how I might order my material for the memoir. I thought about my work, and how I might rearrange my office for the benefit of the people who worked there. These and other related schemes preoccupied me all the way to St. Maurice.

My mood of tranquil self-sufficiency was still with me as I made my way through the village. I drank a beer on the terrace of the Hôtel des Tilleuls, perhaps at the very table where the young honeymooning couple had listened to the mayor over lunch. I booked a room for the night, then set out to walk the mile or so to the dolmen. In order to gain time, I went by the road. A few hundred yards to my right was the lip of the gorge, obscured by a rise in the land, and rolling away to the left and ahead was the harsher landscape of the Causse, hard parched soil, sagebrush, telegraph poles. Just past the ruined farm, La Prunarède, I turned down a sandy track on the right, and five minutes later I was at the dolmen. I took off my pack and sat on the great flat slab and peeled an orange. The stone was barely warm in the afternoon sun. On the way here I had deliberately kept my mind free of intentions, but now I had arrived they seemed clear enough.

Rather than remain the passive victim of my subjects' voices, I had come to pursue them, to re-create Bernard and June sitting here slicing their *saucisson,* crumbling their dried-out bread as they stared north across the gorge at their future: to commune with the optimism of their generation, and to sift June's first doubts on the eve of her confrontation. I wanted to catch them in love, before the lifelong quarrel began.

But I felt purged after my five hours' walk. I was balanced and purposeful and in no mood for ghosts. My mind was still full of my own schemes and projects. I was no longer available for a haunting. The voices had truly gone; there was no one here but me. The low November sun to my right was picking out the shadowy intricacies of the far cliff. I needed nothing more than my pleasure in the place itself and my memories of the family picnics we had had here with Bernard and our children when we had used the big stone slab for our table.

I finished both my oranges and wiped my hands on my shirt, like a schoolboy. I intended to walk back on the track that runs along the edge of the gorge, but in the time since my last visit it had become overgrown with prickly shrubs. After a hundred yards I had to turn back. I was irritated. I had thought I was taking control, and here was an immediate rebuttal. But I calmed myself with the recollection that this was the path to St. Maurice that Bernard and June had taken that evening. That was their way; mine was different—up to the old farm and back along the road. If I had to make a symbol out of an overgrown path, this would suit me better.

·   ·   ·

It had been my intention to end this section of the memoir at this very moment, when I walked back from the dolmen feeling free enough of my subjects to write about them. But I must briefly recount what happened in the hotel restaurant that evening, for it was a drama that seemed to be enacted for me alone. It was an embodiment, however distorted, of my preoccupations, of the loneliness of my childhood; it represented a purging, an exorcism, in which I acted on behalf of my niece, Sally, as well for myself, and took our revenge. Described in June's terms, it was another 'haunting' in which she herself was present, watching me. I certainly took strength from the courage she had shown in her ordeal, one mile away and forty-three years before. Perhaps June would have said that what I really had to confront was within me, since at the very end I was restrained, brought to heel, by words usually spoken to dogs: *Ça suffit!*

I cannot quite remember how it came about, but at some point after my return to the Hôtel des Tilleuls, either when I sat at the bar and drank a Pernod or half an hour later, when I came back down from my room in search of a bar of soap, I learned that the *patronne* was Mme. Monique Auriac, a name I remembered from my notes. She was surely the daughter of the Mme. Auriac who had looked after June, and perhaps she was the young girl who had served lunch while the *Maire* told his story. I thought I would ask her some questions and find out how much she remembered. But the bar was suddenly deserted, and so too was the dining room. I could hear voices in the kitchen. Feeling that the smallness of the establishment somehow excused my transgression, I pushed open the scarred swing doors and stepped through.

In front of me, on a table in a wicker basket, was a heap of bloodied fur. At the far end of the kitchen a row was in progress. Mme. Auriac and her brother, who was the cook, and the girl who doubled as chambermaid and waitress glanced at me and then continued to talk over one another. I stood waiting by the stove, where a pan of soup was simmering. After half a minute I would have tiptoed out and tried later, if I had not begun to realize that the argument concerned me. The hotel was meant to be closed. Because the girl had let the gentleman from England stay—Mme. Auriac gestured toward me with the back of her wrist—she, Mme. Auriac, had been obliged for the sake of consistency to let a family take two rooms, and now a lady from Paris had arrived. How was everyone going to eat? And they were understaffed.

Her brother said that there was no difficulty so long as all the guests ate the seventy-five-franc menu—soup, salad, rabbit, cheese—and did not expect choices. The girl backed him up. Mme. Auriac said that was not the kind of restaurant she wanted to run. At this point I cleared my throat and excused myself and said that I was certain that all the guests were only too happy to find the hotel open so late in the year and that in the circumstances the set menu would be perfectly agreeable. Mme. Auriac left the kitchen with an impatient hissing sound and a toss of the head, which was a form of acceptance, and her brother spread his palms in triumph. One further concession was required; to simplify the work, all the guests should eat early and all together at half past seven. I said that speaking for myself that was quite acceptable, and the cook sent the girl to inform the others.

Half an hour later, I was the first to take my seat in the dining room. I now felt myself something more than a guest.

I was an insider, party to the hotel's internal affairs. Mme. Auriac herself brought me my bread and wine. She was in good humor now and we established that she had indeed been working here in 1946, and though of course she did not remember Bernard and June's visit, she certainly knew the *Maire*'s story about the dogs and she promised to talk to me when she was less busy. Next to appear was the lady from Paris. She was in her early thirties and was beautiful in a drawn, emaciated way, with that brittle, overmanicured appearance some French women have, too arranged, too severe for my taste. She had concave cheeks and the huge eyes of the famished. I guessed she would not be eating much. She clicked across the tiled floor to a far corner, to the table furthest from mine. By ignoring so completely the presence of the sole occupant of the room, she created the paradoxical impression that her every movement was made with me in mind. I had put down the book I was reading and was wondering whether this was in fact the case, or whether it was one of those masculine projections that women sometimes complain about, when the family came in.

There were three of them, husband, wife, and a seven- or eight-year-old boy, and they arrived wrapped in their own silence, a luminous envelope of familial intensity that moved across the larger quietness of the dining room to occupy the next table but one from mine. They sat with a loud scrape of chairs. The man, cock of his tiny roost, rested his tattooed forearms on the table and looked around him. He stared first in the direction of the Parisian lady, who did not—or would not—look up from the menu, and then his eyes met mine. Though I nodded, there was no trace of acknowledgment. He simply registered me, then murmured to his wife, who took from her handbag a packet of Gauloises and a lighter. While the parents lit up, I looked at the boy, who sat alone on his side of the table. My impression was that there had been a scene outside the dining room a few minutes before, some misbehavior for which the child had been reprimanded. He sat listlessly, sulking perhaps, his left hand hanging at his side, his right toying with the cutlery.

Mme. Auriac arrived with bread, water, and the barely drinkable refrigerated liter of red wine. After she had left, the boy slumped further, placing his elbow on the table and propping his head with his hand. Immediately, his mother's hand flashed across the tablecloth and delivered a sharp slap to the boy's forearm, knocking it away. The father, squinting up through his smoke, did not seem to notice. No one spoke. The Parisian woman, whom I could see beyond the family, stared with resolution into an empty corner of the room. The boy slumped against the backrest of his chair, gazing at his lap and rubbing his arm. His mother delicately tapped her cigarette on the ashtray. She hardly looked the hitting sort. She was plump and pink, with a pleasant round face and red patches on her cheeks like a doll's, and this disjunction between her behavior and her maternal appearance was sinister. I felt oppressed by the presence of this family and its miserable situation, about which I could do nothing. If there had been somewhere else in the village to eat, I would have gone there.

I had finished my *lapin au chef* and the family was still eating salad. For some minutes the only sound had been that of cutlery against plates. It was not possible to read, so I watched quietly over the top of my book. The father was screwing pieces of bread into his plate, mopping up the last of the vinaigrette. He lowered his head to take each morsel, as though the hand that fed him were not his. The boy finished by pushing his plate to one side and dabbing his mouth with the back of his hand. It looked like an absentminded gesture, for the boy was a fastidious eater, and as far as I could see, his lips were not smeared with food. But I was an outsider, and perhaps this was a provocation, a continuation of a long-running conflict. His father immediately murmured a phrase that included the word *serviette*. The mother had stopped eating and was watching closely. The boy took his napkin from his lap and pressed it carefully, not to his mouth, but first to one cheek and then the other. In a child so young it could only have been an artless attempt to do the right thing. But his father did not think so. He leaned across the empty salad bowl and pushed the boy hard below the collarbone. The blow jolted the child out of his chair onto the floor. The mother half rose out of her chair and seized his arm. She wanted to get to him before he started howling, and thereby preserve the proprieties of the restaurant. The child hardly knew where he was as she cautioned him in a hiss, *'Tais-toi! Tais-toi!'* Without leaving her seat, she managed to haul him back into the chair, which her husband had righted skillfully with his foot. The couple worked in evident harmony. They seemed to believe that by not standing up they had succeeded in avoiding an unpleasant scene. The boy was back in his place, whimpering. His mother held before him a rigid, cautionary forefinger, and kept it there until he was completely silent. With her eyes still on him, she lowered her hand.

My own hand shook as I poured Mme. Auriac's thin sharp wine. I emptied my glass in gulps. I felt a constriction about my throat. That the boy was not even permitted to cry seemed to me even more terrible than the blow that had knocked him to the floor. It was his loneliness that gripped me. I remembered my own after my parents died, how incommunicable the despair was, how I expected nothing. For this boy, misery was simply the condition of the world. Who could possibly help him? I looked around. The woman sitting alone had her head turned away, but the way she fumbled with the lighting of her cigarette made it clear she had seen everything. At the far end of the dining room, by the buffet, stood the young girl waiting to take our plates. The French are notably kind and tolerant toward children. Surely something was going to be said. Someone, not me, had to intervene.

I downed another glass of wine. A family occupies an inviolable, private space. Behind walls both visible and notional it makes its own rules for its members. The girl came forward and cleared my table. Then she came back to take the salad bowl from the family and bring clean plates. I think I understand what happened to the boy just then. As the table was readied for the next course, as the stewed rabbit was set down, he began to cry; with the coming and going of the waitress came confirmation that after his humiliation, life was to proceed as normal. His sense of isolation was complete and he could not hold back his despair.

First he shook with the attempt to do just that, and then it broke, a nauseous keening sound that grew louder, despite the finger his mother had raised again, then it broadened to a wail, then a sob on a desperate lunging intake of breath. The father put down the fresh cigarette he had been about to light. He paused a moment to discover what would follow the inhalation, and as the child's cry rose, the man's arm made an extravagant sweep across the table and he struck the boy's face with the back of his hand.

It was impossible, I thought I had not seen it—a strong man could not hit a child this way, with the unrestrained force of adult hatred. The child's head snapped back as the blow carried both him and chair he was sitting on almost to my table. It was the chair's back that cracked against the floor and saved the boy's head from damage. The waitress was running toward us, calling for Mme. Auriac as she came. I had made no decision to stand, but I was on my feet. For an instant, I met the gaze of the woman from Paris. She was immobile. Then she nodded gravely. The young waitress had gathered up the child and was sitting on the floor making breathy, flutelike notes of concern over him, a lovely sound, I remember thinking as I arrived at the father's table.

His wife had risen from her seat and was whining to the girl, 'You don't understand, mademoiselle. You'll only make things worse. He'll scream, that one, but he knows what he's up to. He always gets his way.'

There was no sign of Mme. Auriac. Again, I had made no decision, no calculation as to what I was getting myself into. The man had lit his cigarette. It relieved me a little to see that his hands were shaky. He did not look at me. I spoke out in a clear, trembling voice with tolerable accuracy but virtually no idiom. I had none of Jenny's sinuous mastery. Speaking in French elevated both my sentiments and my words into a theatrical, self-conscious solemnity, and standing there, I had a brief ennobling sense of myself as one of those obscure French citizens who blossom from nowhere at a transforming moment in their nation's history to improvise the words that history will engrave in stone. Was this the tennis-court oath?

Was I Desmoulins at the Café Foy? In fact all I said was, literally, 'Monsieur, to hit a child in this way is disgusting. You are an animal, an animal, monsieur. Are you frightened of fighting someone your own size, because I would love to smash my jaw.'

This ridiculous slip of the tongue caused the man to relax. He smiled up at me as he pushed his chair back from the table. He saw a pale Englishman of medium height who still held his napkin in his hand. What did a man have to fear who had a caduceus tattooed on each of his fat forearms?

'Ta gueule? It would make me happy to help you smash it.' He jerked his head toward the door.

I followed him past the empty tables. I could hardly believe it. We were stepping outside. A reckless exhilaration lightened my tread, and I seemed to hover above the restaurant floor. As we went out, the man I had challenged let the swing door fall against me. He led the way across the deserted road to where a petrol pump stood under a streetlamp. He turned to face me and square up, but I had already made up my mind, and even as he raised his arms my fist was traveling toward his face with all my weight behind it. I caught him hard and full on the nose with such force that even as his bone crunched, I felt something snap in my knuckle. There was a satisfying moment when he was stunned but could not fall. His arms dropped to his sides and he stood there and watched me as I hit him with the left, one two three, face, throat, and gut, before he went down. I drew back my foot, and I think I might have kicked and stomped him to death if I had not heard a voice and turned to see a thin figure in the lighted doorway across the road.

The voice was calm. *'Monsieur. Je vous prie. Ça suffit.'*

Immediately I knew that the elation driving me had nothing to do with revenge and justice. Horrified with myself, I stepped back.

I crossed the road and followed the woman from Paris inside. While we waited for the police and an ambulance, Mme. Auriac bound my hand with a bandage and went behind the bar to pour me a cognac. And at the bottom of the fridge she found the last of the summer's ice cream for the boy, who still sat on the floor recovering, wrapped in the maternal arms of the pretty young waitress, who, it must be said, appeared flushed and in the embrace of a great happiness.

4

· · · · · · · · · · · · · · ·

St. Maurice
de Navacelles,
1946

In the spring of 1946, taking advantage of a newly liberated Europe and favorable exchange rates, my parents-in-law, Bernard and June Tremaine, set off on a honeymoon tour of France and Italy. They had met in 1944 in Senate House, Bloomsbury, where they both worked. My wife's father, a Cambridge science graduate, had a desk job peripherally connected with the intelligence services. It had something to do with the supply of special items. My mother-in-law was a linguist working in an office that liaised with, or as she used to put it, smoothed out the rumpled feelings of, the Free French. She occasionally found herself in the same room as de Gaulle. It was translation work for a project involving the adaptation of treadle sewing machines to power generation that brought her to the office of her future husband. They were not given permission to leave their jobs until almost a year after the war ended. They were married in April. The idea was to spend the summer traveling before settling down to peacetime, married life, and civilian work.

In the years when these things mattered more to me, I used to reflect a great deal on the different war work available to people of different classes, and on this lively assumption of choice, this youthful desire to experience new freedoms, which as far as I know hardly touched my own parents' lives. They also married soon after the war ended. My mother had been a land girl, working on farms as part of the war effort, which she hated, according to one of my aunts. In 1943 she transferred to work in a munitions factory near Colchester. My father was in the infantry. He survived intact the evacuation from Dunkirk, fought in North Africa, and finally met his bullet during the Normandy landings. It passed clean through his right hand without harming a bone. My parents could have traveled after the war. Apparently they inherited a few hundred pounds from my grandfather at just about the time my father was demobilized. Theoretically, they were free to go, but I doubt if it occurred to them, or to any of their friends. I used to think it one more aspect of the narrowness of my background that the money was used to buy the terraced house in which my sister and I were born, and to launch the hardware business that supported us after our parents' sudden death.

Now I think I understand a little more. My father-in-law spent his working hours on problems like silent power generation for the operation of radio transmitters in remote French farmhouses where there was no electricity supply. In the evenings he went back to his rooms and dull wartime diet in Finchley, and at weekends he visited his parents in Cobham. Later in the war there was his courtship, with cinema visits and Sunday hikes in the Chilterns. Set against this the life of an infantry sergeant: enforced travel abroad, boredom alternating with severe stress, the violent deaths and terrible injuries of close friends, no privacy, no women, irregular news from home. The prospect of a life of constrained and rhythmic ordinariness must have acquired, in the slow slog eastward through Belgium with a throbbing hand, a glow quite unknown to my parents-in-law.

Understanding these differences does not make them any more attractive, and I have always known whose war I would rather have had. The honeymooning couple arrived in the Italian seaside town of Lerici in mid-June. The chaos and devastation of postwar Europe, especially in northern France and Italy, had shocked them. They offered themselves for six weeks' voluntary work in a Red Cross packing station on the outskirts of the town. It was dull, arduous labor, and the hours were long. People were exhausted, preoccupied with daily issues of survival, and no one seemed to care that this was a couple on honeymoon. Their immediate boss, *il capo*, took against them. He bore a grudge against the British that he was too proud to discuss. They lodged with Signor and Signore Massimo, who were still grieving for their two sons, their only children, killed in the same week, fifty miles apart, just before the Italian surrender. Some nights the English couple were woken by the elderly parents downstairs weeping together over their loss.

The food ration, on paper at least, was adequate, but local corruption kept it to a minimum. Bernard developed a skin complaint which spread from his hands to his throat and across his face. June was propositioned daily, despite the brass curtain ring she wore specially. Men were constantly standing too close, or rubbing against her as they passed in the gloom of the packing shed, or tweaking her behind or the bare skin of her forearm. The problem, the other women told her, was her fair hair.

They could have left at any time, but the Tremaines stuck it out. This was their small atonement for their comfortable war. It was also an expression of their idealism; it was 'winning the peace' and helping to 'build a new Europe.' But their departure from Lerici was rather sad. No one noticed their going. The grieving Italians were ministering to a dying parent on the top floor and the house had filled with relatives. The Red Cross station was absorbed by an embezzlement scandal. Bernard and June slipped away before dawn one morning in early August to wait out on the main road for the bus that would take them north to Genoa. As they stood there in the half-light, depressed and hardly speaking, they would surely have felt cheered about their contribution to a new Europe to have known that they had already conceived their first child, a daughter, my wife, who would one day put up a good fight for a seat in the European parliament.

They traveled by bus and train westward through Provence, through flash floods and electrical storms. In Arles they met a French government official who drove them to

Lodève in Languedoc. He told them that if they presented themselves at his hotel in a week's time, he would take them on with him to Bordeaux. The skies had cleared, they were not due in England for another two weeks, and so they set off on a short walking tour.

This is the region where the Causses, high limestone plateaus, rise a thousand feet above the coastal plain. In places the cliffs drop spectacularly hundreds of feet. Lodève stands at the foot of one of the passes, then a narrow country road, now the busy RN 9. It is still a fine ascent, though with such traffic, hardly pleasant on foot. In those days you could pass a tranquil day climbing steadily between towering formations of rock until you could see the Mediterranean shining behind you, thirty miles to the south. The Tremaines spent the night at the small town of Le Caylar, where they bought broad-brimmed shepherd's hats. The next morning they left the road and headed off northeast across the Causse de Larzac, carrying two liters of water each.

These are some of the emptiest spaces in France. There are fewer people here now than there were a hundred years ago. Dusty tracks, unmarked on the best of maps, wind across expanses of heather, gorse, and box. Deserted farms and hamlets sit in hollows of surprising greenness, where small pastures are divided by ancient dry stone walls and the paths between them, flanked by tall blackberry bushes, wild roses, and oaks, have an English intimacy. But these soon give way to the emptiness again.

Toward the end of the day the Tremaines came across the Dolmen de la Prunarède, a prehistoric burial chamber. Then, only several yards farther on, they found themselves standing above a deep gorge carved through the rock by the

River Vis. They stopped here to finish off their provisions—huge tomatoes of a kind never seen in England, two-day-old bread as dry as a biscuit, and a *saucisson,* which June sliced with Bernard's penknife. They had been silent for hours, and now, sitting on the dolmen's horizontal slab of stone, gazing north across the chasm to the Causse de Blandas and beyond to where the Cévennes mountains rise, an excited discussion began in which their route the next day across this glorious alien countryside became one with their sense of their lives before them. Bernard and June were members of the Communist party, and they were talking of the way ahead. For hours, intricate domestic details, the baby, distances between villages, choices of footpaths, the routing of fascism, class struggle, and the great engine of history, whose direction was now known to science and which had granted to the party its inalienable right to govern, all merged in one spectacular view, a beckoning avenue unrolling from the starting point of their love, out across the vast prospect of Causse and mountains, which reddened as they spoke, then darkened. And as the dusk gathered, so too did June's disquiet. Was she losing the faith already? An ageless silence was tempting her, drawing her in, but whenever she ceased her own optimistic prattle to attend to it, the void was filled with Bernard's sonorous platitudes, the militarized vacuities, the 'front,' the 'attack,' the 'enemies' of Marxist-Leninist thought.

June's blasphemous uncertainties were only temporarily dispelled when the two lingered on their walk through the evening to the nearby village of St. Maurice to conclude, or extend, their discussion of the future by making love, perhaps on the track itself, where the ground was softest. But the next day, and the day after, and on all the succeeding days, they never set foot in the metaphorical landscape of their future. The next day they turned back. They never descended the Gorge de Vis and walked by the mysterious raised canal that disappears into the rock, never crossed the river by the medieval bridge or climbed up to cross the Causse de Blandas and wander among the prehistoric menhirs, cromlechs, and dolmens scattered in the wilderness, never began the long ascent of the Cévennes toward Florac. The next day they began their separate journeys.

In the morning they set out from the Hôtel des Tilleuls in St. Maurice. As they crossed the pretty stretch of pasture and gorseland that separates the village from the edge of the gorge, they were silent again. It was barely nine o'clock and already too hot. For a quarter of an hour they lost the path and had to cut across a field. The din of cicadas, the aromatic dry grasses crushed underfoot, the ferocious sun in its sky of innocent pale blue—all that had seemed so exotically southern the day before was troubling to June today. It bothered her that she was walking farther away from their luggage in Lodève. In the sharp light of morning, the arid horizon, the dry mountains ahead, the miles they would have to cover that day to reach the town of Le Vigan, were weighing on her. The days of walking ahead of them seemed a pointless detour from her uncertainty.

She was thirty feet or so behind Bernard, whose shambling stride was as confident as his opinions. She took refuge in guilty, bourgeois thoughts of the house they would buy in England, a scrubbed kitchen table, the simple blue-and-white china her mother had given her, the baby. Ahead they could see the dreadful sheer cliff of the gorge's northern edge. The land was already dropping slightly; the vegetation was changing. Instead of carefree joy she felt a sourceless fear, too faint to be complained of aloud. It was an agoraphobia, mediated, perhaps, by the tiny growth, the rapidly dividing cells driving Jenny into existence.

Turning back on the basis of a slight, nameless anxiety was out of the question. The day before they had agreed that here at last was the fulfillment of their months abroad. The weeks in the Red Cross packing shed behind them, the English winter ahead, why was she not rejoicing in this sunlit freedom, what was wrong with her?

Where the path began its steep descent, they stopped to marvel at the prospect. On the far side, facing them across half a mile of bright, empty space, was a vertical wall of baking rock dropping three hundred feet. Here and there hardy scrub oaks had found purchase and a little soil in fissures and on ledges. This mad vigor that forced life to cling in the harshest of places wearied June. She experienced a deep nausea. A thousand feet down was the river, lost among the trees. The empty air, suffused with sunlight, seemed to contain a darkness just beyond the reach of vision.

She was standing on the path exchanging murmurs of appreciation. The earth nearby had been trodden flat by other walkers stopping to do the same. Mere pieties. The proper response was fear. She half remembered reading the accounts of eighteenth-century travelers in the Lake District and the Swiss Alps. Mountain peaks were terrifying, plummeting gorges were horrible, untamed nature was a chaos, a postlapsarian rebuke, a dread reminder.

Her hand was resting lightly on Bernard's shoulder, her

rucksack was on the ground between her feet, and she was talking to persuade herself, listening to be persuaded, that what lay before them was exhilarating, was somehow in its very naturalness an embodiment, a reflection of their human goodness. But of course by its dryness alone, this place was their enemy. Everything that grew was tough, scrubby, prickly, hostile to the touch, preserving its fluids in the bitter cause of survival. She took her hand off Bernard's shoulder and reached down for her water bottle. She could not speak her fear because it seemed so unreasonable. Every definition of herself she groped for in her discomfort urged her to enjoy the view and get on with the walk: a mother-to-be in love with her husband, a socialist and optimist, compassionately rational, free of superstitions, on a walking tour in the country of her specialty, redeeming the long years of the duration and dull weeks in Italy, seizing the last days of carefree holiday before England, responsibility, winter.

She pushed aside her fear and began to talk with enthusiasm. And yet she knew from the map that the river crossing at Navacelles was miles upstream and that the descent would take two or three hours. They would be making the shorter, steeper climb out of the gorge in the midday heat. All afternoon they would be crossing the Causse de Blandas, which she could see on the other side, basking in its heat warp. She needed all her strength, and she summoned it by talking. She heard herself compare the Gorge de Vis favorably with the Golfe de Verdon in Provence. As she talked she redoubled her jolliness, though she hated every gorge, ravine, and rift in the world and she wanted to go home.

Then Bernard was talking as they picked up their rucksacks and got ready to set off again. His big, stubbly, good-natured face and protruding ears were sunburned. His dried skin gave him a dusty appearance. How could she let him down? He was talking of a ravine in Crete. He had heard there was a magnificent spring walk to be made among the wildflowers. Perhaps they should try to go next year. She was walking on a few paces ahead of him, nodding ostentatiously.

She thought that she was experiencing no more than a passing mood, a difficulty in getting started, and that the rhythm of walking would settle her. By the evening, in the hotel at Le Vigan, her anxieties would have shrunk to an anecdote; over a glass of wine, they would appear as one element in a varied day. The path was making leisurely zigzags across a broad shoulder of sloping land. Its surface was easy underfoot. She angled her broad-brimmed hat jauntily against the sun and swung her arms as she loped on down. She heard Bernard call after her and chose to ignore him. Perhaps she even thought that by striding on ahead she could somehow dishearten him, so that he would be the one to suggest turning back.

She came to a hairpin bend in the track and turned it. A hundred yards ahead, by the next bend, were two donkeys. The path was broader here, fringed by shrubs of box that looked planted out, they were so regularly spaced. She caught a glimpse of something interesting farther down, and she leaned over the edge of the path to look. It was an old irrigation canal built of stone and set into the side of the gorge. She could see the path alongside it. In half an hour they would be able to splash their faces and cool their wrists. As she came away from the edge she looked ahead again and realized that the donkeys were dogs, black dogs of an unnatural size.

She did not stop immediately. The coldness spreading from her stomach down through her legs numbed any immediate response. Instead, she slowed falteringly, taking half a dozen steps before she stood motionless and unbalanced in the center of the path. They had not seen her yet. She knew little about dogs, and she had no great fear of them. Even the frantic animals around the remote farmsteads on the Causse had worried her only a little. But the creatures that blocked the path seventy yards ahead were dogs only in outline. In size they resembled mythical beasts. The suddenness of them, the anomaly, prompted the thought of a message in dumb show, an allegory for her decipherment alone. She had a confusing thought of something medieval, of a tableau both formal and terrifying. At this distance the animals appeared to be grazing quietly. They emanated meaning. She felt weak and sick in her fear. She was waiting for the sound of Bernard's footsteps. Surely she had not been so far ahead of him.

In this landscape, where the working animals were small and wiry, there was no use for dogs the size of donkeys. These creatures—giant mastiffs perhaps—were sniffing around a patch of grass by the side of the path. They were without collars, without an owner. They moved slowly. They seemed to be working together to some purpose. Their blackness, that they should both be black, that they belonged together and were without an owner, made her think of apparitions. June did not believe in such things. She was drawn to the idea now because the creatures were familiar. They were emblems of the menace she had felt, they were the embodiment of the nameless, unreasonable, unmentionable disquiet she had felt that morning. She did not believe in ghosts. But she did believe in madness. What she feared more than the presence of the dogs was the possibility of their absence, of their not existing at all. One of the dogs, slightly smaller than its mate, looked up and saw her.

That the animals could behave independently of each other seemed to confirm their existence in the real world. This was no comfort. While the larger dog continued to nose in the grass, the other stood quite still, one front paw raised, and looked at her, or breathed her scent in the warm air. June had grown up on the edge of the countryside, but she was a city girl really. She knew enough not to run, but she was an office, library, cinema sort of girl. In twenty-six years she had had an average share of danger. A V-bomb had once exploded three hundred yards from where she was sheltering; during the early days of the blackout she had been a passenger on a bus that had collided with a motorbike; when she was nine she had fallen into a weedy pond with all her clothes on, in midwinter. The memory of these adventures, or the flavor of all three distilled into one metallic essence, came to her now. The dog advanced a few yards and stopped. Its tail was low, the front feet were planted firmly. June stepped backward, one step, then another two. Her left leg was trembling in the knee joint. The right was better. She imagined the creature's visual field: a colorless wash and one blurred hovering perpendicular, unmistakably human, edible.

She was certain that these ownerless dogs would be famished. Out here, two miles or more from St. Maurice, even a hunting dog would have a hard time of it. These were guard dogs, bred for aggression, not survival. Or pets that had outgrown their charm or were costing too much to feed. June stepped back again. She was afraid, reasonably afraid, not of dogs but of the unnatural size of these particular dogs in this remote place. And of their color? No, not that. The second, larger dog saw her and came forward to stand by its mate. They remained still for a quarter of a minute, then they began to walk toward her. If they had broken into a run, she would have been helpless before them. But she needed to watch them all the time, she had to see them coming. She risked a glance behind her; the snapshot of the sunlit path was vividly empty of Bernard.

He was more than three hundred yards away. He had stopped to retie his lace and had become engrossed by the progress, inches from the tip of his shoe, of a caravan of two dozen brown furry caterpillars, each with its mandibles clamped to the rear of the one in front. He had called to June, wanting her to come back and look, but by then she had already rounded the first bend. Bernard's scientific curiosity was aroused. The procession along the path looked purposeful. He wanted to know exactly where it was going, and what would happen when it arrived. He was on his knees with his box camera. Nothing much showed through the viewfinder. He took a notebook from his rucksack and began to make a sketch.

The dogs were less than fifty yards away, and coming at a fast walk. When they got to her they would be waist high, perhaps bigger. Their tails were down and their mouths were open. June could see their pink tongues. Nothing else in this hard landscape was pink apart from her tender sunburned legs, exposed below her baggy shorts. For comfort she tried to force a memory of an ancient Lakeland terrier belonging to an aunt, of how it ambled across the rectory hallway, toenails clipping the polished oak boards, to greet each new visitor, neither friendly nor hostile but dutifully inquisitive. There was a certain irreducible respect owed by dogs to humans, bred over generations, founded upon the unquestionable facts of human intelligence and dog stupidity. And on dogs' celebrated loyalty, their dependency, their abject desire to be mastered. But out here the rules were exposed as mere convention, a flimsy social contract. Here, no institutions asserted human ascendancy. There was only the path, which belonged to any creature that could walk it.

The dogs kept to their mutinous advance. June was walking backward. She dared not run. She shouted Bernard's name once, twice, three times. Her voice sounded thin in the sunny air. It caused the dogs to come faster, almost at a trot. She must not show her fear. But they would smell it on her. She must not feel her fear, then. Her hands shook as she scrabbled on the path for rocks. She found three. She held one in her right hand and kept the others wedged between her left hand and her side. She was retreating sideways, keeping her left shoulder toward the dogs. Where the path dipped, she stumbled and fell. In her anxiety to be on her feet again, she almost bounced off the ground.

She still had the rocks. Her forearm was cut. Would the smell of the wound excite them? She wanted to suck the blood away, but to do that she would have to let the rocks fall. There were still more than a hundred yards to the bend in the path. The dogs were twenty yards away and closing. She drifted apart from her body when she stopped at last and turned to face them; this detached self was prepared to watch with indifference—worse, acceptance—a young woman being eaten alive. She noted with contempt the whimper on each outbreath, and how a muscular spasm was causing the left leg to tremble so much it could no longer bear weight.

She leaned back against a small oak that overhung the path. She felt her rucksack between her and the tree. Without dropping her stones, she eased it off her shoulders and held it before her. At fifteen feet the dogs stopped. She realized she had been clinging to the one last hope that her fear was no more than silliness. She realized it the moment the hope dissolved in the smooth rumble of the larger dog's growl. The smaller one was flattened against the ground, front legs tensed, ready to spring. Its mate circled slowly to the left, keeping its distance, until it was only possible to hold them both in her field of vision by letting her eyes flicker between them. In this way she saw them as a juddering accumulation of disjointed details: the alien black gums, slack black lips rimmed by salt, a thread of saliva breaking, the fissures on a tongue that ran to smoothness along its curling edge, a yellow-red eye and eyeball muck spiking the fur, open sores on a foreleg, and, trapped in the V of an open mouth, deep in the hinge of the jaw, a little foam, to which her gaze kept returning. The dogs had brought with them their own cloud of flies. Some of them now defected to her.

Bernard did not derive pleasure from sketching, nor did his drawings resemble what he saw. They represented what he knew, or wanted to know. They were diagrams, or maps, onto which he would later transcribe missing names. If he could identify the caterpillar, it would be easy to find out from reference books what it was up to, if he failed to discover for himself today. He had depicted a caterpillar as a scaled-up oblong. Close examination had shown that they were not brown but striped in subtle shades of orange and black. He had shown only one set of stripes on his diagram, drawn in careful proportion to the length, with penciled arrows indicating colors. He had counted the members of the caravan—not so easy when each individual merged into the fur of the next. He recorded twenty-eight. He drew a head-on view of the leader's face, showing the relative size and disposition of the jaws and compound eyes. As he had knelt down, his cheek grazing the path, to stare up close at the head of the leading caterpillar, at a hinged face of inscrutable parts, he had thought how we share the planet with creatures as weird and as alien to us as any that could be imagined from outer space. But we give them names and stop seeing them, or their size prevents us from looking. He reminded himself to pass this thought on to June, who even now would be walking back up the path to find him, possibly a little cross.

She was addressing the dogs, in English, then in French. She spoke forcefully to hold down the sickness. In the confident tone of a dog owner she commanded the larger dog, which stood with its front legs set apart, still growling.

'*Ça suffit!*'

It did not hear. It did not blink. On her right, its companion eased forward on its belly. If they had barked she would have felt better. The silences that interrupted the growls suggested calculation. The animals had a plan. From the jaws of the larger dog a drop of saliva fell onto the path. Several flies were on it in an instant.

June whispered, 'Please go away. Please. Oh God!' The expletive brought her to the conventional thought of her last and best chance. She tried to find the space within her for the presence of God and thought she discerned the faintest of outlines, a significant emptiness she had never noticed before, at the back of her skull. It seemed to lift and flow upward and outward, streaming suddenly into an oval penumbra many feet high, an envelope of rippling energy, or, as she tried to explain it later, of 'colored invisible light' that surrounded her and contained her. If this was God, it was also, incontestably, herself. Could it help her? Would this Presence be moved by a sudden, self-interested conversion? An appeal, a whimpering prayer to something that was so clearly, so luminously an extension of her own being, seemed irrelevant. Even in this moment of extremity she knew she had discovered something extraordinary, and she was determined to survive and investigate it.

Still holding the rock, she slipped her right hand into her rucksack. She pulled out the remains of the *saucisson* they had been eating the day before, and tossed it to the ground. The smaller dog was there first, but ceded to its mate immediately. The sausage and its greaseproof paper were down in less than thirty seconds. The dog turned to her, drooling. A triangular shred of paper was trapped between two teeth. The bitch nosed the ground where the sausage had been. June returned her hand to the rucksack. She felt something hard between the bundles of folded clothes. She drew out a penknife with a bakelite handle. The larger dog took two quick steps toward her. It was ten feet away. She transferred the rock to her left hand, put the bakelite in her mouth, and opened out the knife. She could not hold it and the rock in one hand. There was a choice to be made. The knife with its three-inch blade was a last resort. She could use it only when the dogs were on her. She balanced it on top of the rucksack, handle pointing toward her. She took the rock in her right hand again and pushed back against the tree. Her terrified grip had warmed the rock through. She drew back her hand. Now that she was about to attack, her left leg was shaking more.

The rock hit the ground hard and sent a spray of smaller stones across the path. She missed the larger dog by a foot. It flinched when the stones rose into its face, but it held its ground and lowered its nose to the place of impact, still hoping for food. When it looked at her again it twisted its head to one side and snarled, a nasty breath-and-mucus sound. It was as she had feared. She had raised the stakes. Another rock was in her hand. The bitch flattened its ears and slipped forward. Her throw was wild, hopeless. The rock spun out of her hand too soon. It fell feebly to one side and her unweighted arm thrashed the air.

The big dog was down, ready for the spring, waiting for one moment's inattention. The muscles in its haunches quivered. A back paw scrabbled for better purchase. She had seconds left, and her hand was around her third rock. It went over the dog's back and hit the path. The sound caused the dog to half turn, and in that instant, in that extra second, June moved. She had nothing to lose. In a delirium of abandonment, she attacked. She had passed through fear to fury that her happiness, the hopes of the past months, and now the revelation of this extraordinary light were about to be destroyed by a pair of abandoned dogs. She took the knife in her right hand and held the rucksack like a shield and rushed the dogs, shrieking a terrible *aaaaaaa!*

The bitch leapt back. But the big one went for her. It sprang up. She leaned forward to meet the impact as the animal sank its jaws into the rucksack. It was on its hind legs and she was supporting it with one arm. She was buckling under the weight. The dog's face was inches above hers. She thrust upward with the knife, three quick jabs to its belly and sides. It surprised her, how easily the blade went in. A good little knife. On the first stroke the dog's yellow-red eyes widened. On the second and third, before it let the rucksack go, it made high-pitched piteous yips, a small dog's noise. Encouraged by the sound and screaming again, June lunged upward a fourth time. But the animal's weight was in retreat and she missed. The swing of her arm threw her off balance. She sprawled forward, face down on the path.

The knife had left her hand. The back of her neck was exposed. She hunched her shoulders in a prolonged, trembling shrug, she drew in her arms and legs and covered her face in her hands. *It can come now,* was her only thought. *It can come.*

But it did not. When she dared lift her head, she saw the dogs a hundred yards away and still running, back the way they had come. Then they rounded the corner and were gone.

Bernard found her a quarter of an hour later sitting on the path. When he helped her to her feet, she said tersely that she had been frightened by two dogs and she wanted to turn back. He did not see the bloodied knife, and June forgot to pick it up. He started to tell her how foolish it would be to miss the beautiful descent to Navacelles, and that he could deal with the dogs himself. But June was already walking away. She was not one to force sudden decisions like this. When he picked up her rucksack he saw a curving row of punctures in the canvas and a streak of foam, but he was too intent on catching up with June. When he did, she shook her head. She had nothing more to say.

Bernard pulled on her arm to make her stop. 'Let's discuss it, at least. This is a radical change of plan, you know.' He could see she was upset and he was trying to keep his irritation under control. She pulled free and walked on. There was something mechanical in her step. Bernard caught up with her again, puffing from the weight of two bags.

'Something's happened.'

Her silence was assent.

'For God's sake tell me what it is.'

'I can't.' She was still walking on.

Bernard shouted, 'June! This is outrageous!'

'Don't ask me to talk. Help me get to St. Maurice, Bernard. Please.'

She did not wait for a reply. She was not going to argue. He had never known her like this. He suddenly decided to do as she asked. They walked back to the top of the gorge and crossed the pasture in the gathering violence of the heat, toward the tower of the village château.

At the Hôtel des Tilleuls, June mounted the steps to the terrace and sat in the broken shade of the lime trees, gripping with both hands the edge of a painted tin table as though hanging from a cliff. Bernard sat across from her and was drawing breath to ask his first question when she raised her hands, palms outward, and shook her head. They ordered *citrons pressés*. While they waited, Bernard told her about the caterpillar train in some detail, and remembered his observation about the alien nature of other species. June sometimes nodded, though not always at the right moments.

Mme. Auriac, the owner, brought their drinks. She was a busy, maternal lady whom they had christened Mrs. Tiggywinkle the night before. She had lost her husband in 1940 when the Germans crossed the border from Belgium. When she had heard that the couple were English and on honeymoon, she had moved them to a room with a bathroom, at no extra cost. She carried on a tray the glasses of lemon juice, a glass pitcher of water with its Ricard sign, and a saucer of honey in place of sugar, which was still rationed. She sensed that something was not right with June, because she set down her glass with care. Then, an instant before Bernard did, she saw June's right hand, and, mistaking the blood there, took it in her own and exclaimed, 'That's a bad cut, you poor wee thing. You come inside with me and I'll take care of that for you.'

June was docile. Mme. Auriac held her hand as she stood. She was about to allow herself to be led away into the hotel when her face twitched and she let out a strange high note, like a cry of surprise. Bernard was on his feet, appalled, thinking he was about to witness a birth, a miscarriage, some spectacular feminine disaster. Mme. Auriac was steadier and caught the young Englishwoman and eased her back into her chair. June was overcome by a series of arid, stuttering sobs, which broke finally into wet, childlike crying.

When she was able to speak again, June told her story. She sat close to Mme. Auriac, who had called for cognac. Bernard held June's hand across the table, but she would not take comfort from him at first. She had not forgiven him for his absence at a critical time, and the description of his ridiculous caterpillars had kept her resentment alive. But when she came to the climax of her tale and saw his expression of astonishment and pride, she interlocked her fingers with his and returned his loving squeeze.

Mme. Auriac told the waiter to fetch the *Maire,* even if he had started his afternoon sleep. Bernard embraced June and congratulated her on her daring. The cognac was warming her stomach. For the first time she realized that her experience was complete; it was at worst a vivid memory. It was a story, one that she came out of well. In her relief she remembered her love for dear Bernard, so that by the time the *Maire* came up the steps to the terrace, unshaven and groggy from his interrupted nap, he came upon a happy, celebratory scene, a little idyll, with Mme. Auriac smiling on. Naturally enough he was irritable in his demand to know what had been so urgent as to drag him out of his bed into the early afternoon sunlight.

Mme. Auriac appeared to have some power over the *Maire.* When he had shaken hands with the English couple, he was told to sit himself down. He grumpily acquiesced to a cognac. He cheered up when Madame had the waiter bring a pot of coffee to the table. Real coffee was still a scarce commodity. This was from the finest dark Arabian beans. The *Maire* raised his glass a third time. *Vous êtes anglais?* Ah, his son, who was now studying engineering in Clermont-Ferrand, had fought alongside the British Expeditionary Force, and always said—

'Hector, that's for later,' Mme. Auriac said. 'Here there is a grave situation,' and to save June the effort of repetition, she told the story on her behalf, with only minor embellishments. However, when Mme. Auriac had June wrestling with the dog prior to stabbing it, June felt she had to intervene.

The villagers waved this interruption down as irrelevant modesty.

At the end Mme. Auriac showed off June's rucksack. The *Maire* whistled through his teeth and gave his verdict. '*C'est grave.*' Two wild, hungry dogs, possibly rabid, one of them irritable from its wounds, were certainly a public menace. As soon as he had finished this drink he would round up some locals and send them down the gorge to track the animals and shoot them. He would also phone down to Navacelles to see what could be done from that end.

The *Maire* appeared to be about to stand. Then he reached for his empty glass and settled back in his chair.

'We had this once before,' he said. 'Last winter. Remember?'

'I didn't hear about it,' Mme. Auriac said.

'It was one dog last time. But same thing, same reason.'

'Reason?' Bernard asked.

'You mean you didn't know. Ah, *c'est une histoire.*' He pushed his glass toward Mme. Auriac, who called out to the bar. The waiter came and murmured in Mme. Auriac's ear. At a gesture from her he drew up a chair for himself. Suddenly Mme. Auriac's daughter, Monique, who worked in the kitchen, appeared with a tray. They lifted the glasses and cups so that she could spread out a white tablecloth and set down two bottles of *vin de pays,* glasses, a basket of bread, a bowl of olives, and a handful of cutlery. Out in the vineyards, beyond the shady *terrasse,* the cicadas intensified their hot dry sound. Now time, afternoon time, which in the Midi is as elemental as air and light, expanded and rolled billowingly outward across the rest of the day and upward to the vaults of the cobalt sky, freeing everyone in its delicious sprawl from their obligations.

Monique returned with a *terrine de porc* in a glazed brown dish just as the *Maire,* who had filled the fresh glasses with wine, was beginning.

'This was a quiet village at first—I'm talking of 'forty and 'forty-one. We were slow to organize, and for reasons of, well, history, family disputes, stupid arguments, we were left out of a group forming around Madière, the village along the river. But then in 'forty-two, March or April, some of us helped make the Antoinette line. It ran up from the coast around Sète, across the Séranne, through here, into the Cévennes, and on up to Clermont. It cut across the east-west Philippe line to the Pyrénées and Spain.'

The *Maire,* misreading Bernard's consciously blank expression and the fact that June was staring at her lap, offered a quick explanation.

'I'll tell you the kind of thing. Our first job, for example. Radio transmitters brought in by submarine to Cap d'Agde. Our section moved them from La Vacquerie to Le Vigan in three nights. Where they went after that we didn't want to know. You understand?'

Bernard nodded eagerly, as though suddenly everything was clear. June kept her eyes down. They had never discussed their war work together, and were not to do so until 1974. Bernard had organized inventories for numerous drops along different routes, though he had never been directly involved with so minor a line as Antoinette. June had worked for a group liaising with the Free French on SOE policy in Vichy France, but she too knew nothing about Antoinette.

Throughout the *Maire*'s story, Bernard and June avoided each other's eyes.

'Antoinette worked well,' the *Maire* said, 'for seven months. There was only a handful of us here. We passed agents and their radio operators north. Sometimes it was just supplies. We helped a Canadian pilot to the coast . . .'

A restlessness on the part of Mme. Auriac and the waiter suggested that they had heard this too many times before over the cognac bottle, or that they thought the *Maire* was boasting. Mme. Auriac was talking in a low voice to Monique, giving instructions about the next course.

'And then,' the *Maire* said, raising his voice, 'something went wrong. Somebody talked. Two were arrested in Arboras. That was when the Milice came.'

The waiter turned his head politely and spat at the base of a lime tree.

'They went right along the line, set themselves up indoors here at the hotel, and interrogated the whole village one by one. It makes me proud to say they found nothing, absolutely nothing, and they went away. But that was the end of Antoinette, and from then on St. Maurice was under suspicion. Suddenly, it was understood that we controlled a route north across the gorge. We were no longer obscure. They were through here night and day. They recruited informers. Antoinette was dead and it was difficult to start again. The Maquis de Cévennes sent a man down here and there was an argument. We were isolated, that was true, but we were also easy to watch, and the Maquis didn't understand. We have the Causse at our back, with no cover. In front there's the gorge, with only a few routes down.

'But in the end we started up again, and almost immediately our Docteur Boubal was arrested here. They took him all the way to Lyon. He was tortured, and we think he died before he talked. The day he went, the Gestapo arrived. They came with dogs, huge ugly animals they'd been using in the mountains to track down the Maquis hideaways. That was the story, but I never believed they were tracker dogs. They were guard dogs, not bloodhounds. The Gestapo came with these dogs, requisitioned a house in the center of the village, and stayed for three days. It wasn't clear what they wanted. They went away, and ten days later they were back. And two weeks after that. They moved around the area, and we never knew when or where they'd turn up next. They made themselves very public with these dogs, poking into everyone's business. The idea was intimidation, and it worked. Everyone was terrified of these dogs and their handlers. From our point of view, it was difficult to move about at night, with the dogs patroling the village. And by this time the Milice informers were firmly in place.'

The *Maire* emptied his wine in two long pulls and refilled his glass.

'Then we discovered the real purpose of these dogs, or at least, of one of them.'

'Hector . . .' Mme. Auriac warned. 'Not this.'

'First,' the *Maire* said, 'I must tell you something about Danielle Bertrand—'

'Hector,' Mme. Auriac said, 'the young lady does not wish to hear this story.' But whatever power she had over the *Maire* had been lost to the drink.

'It is not possible to say,' he announced, 'that Mme. Bertrand was ever popular here.'

'Thanks to you and your friends,' Mme. Auriac said quietly.

'She came after the war started and took over a small place she had inherited from her aunt on the edge of the village. She said her husband had been killed near Lille in 1940, and that might or might not have been true.'

Mme. Auriac was shaking her head. She was sitting back in her chair with her arms folded.

'We were suspicious. Perhaps we were wrong . . .'

The *Maire* offered this to Mme. Auriac, but she would not look at him. Her disapproval was taking the form of furious silence.

'But that's how it is in war,' he went on, with an open flourish of the hand to suggest that this really would be Mme. Auriac's line, if only she were to speak. 'A stranger coming to live with us, a woman, and no one knew how she got her money, and no one remembering old Mme. Bertrand ever mentioning a niece, and she so aloof, sitting all day in her kitchen with piles of books. Of course we were suspicious. We didn't like her and that was that. And I say all this because I want you to understand, madame'—this to June—'that despite everything I've said, I was horrified by the events of April 1944. It was a matter for deep regret . . .'

Mme. Auriac made a snorting sound. 'Regret!'

At that moment Monique arrived with a large earthenware *cassole,* and for a quarter of an hour attention passed properly to the cassoulet, with statements of appreciation from everyone present, and Mme. Auriac, gratified, responding with the story of how she came by an essential ingredient, the preserved goose.

When the meal was finished, the *Maire* resumed. 'There

were three or four of us sitting at this very table one evening after work when we saw Mme. Bertrand running up the road toward us. She was in a bad way. Her clothes were torn, her nose was bleeding, and she had a cut above her eyebrow. She was shouting—no, she was gibbering, and she ran up here, up those steps, and inside to look for Madame—'

Mme. Auriac said quickly, 'She had been raped by the Gestapo. Excuse me, madame,' and she placed her hand on June's.

'That was what we all thought,' the *Maire* said.

Mme. Auriac raised her voice. 'And that was correct.'

'It's not what we discovered later. Pierre and Henri Sauvy—'

'Drunks!'

'They saw it happen. Excuse me, madame'—to June—'but they tied Danielle Bertrand over a chair.'

Mme. Auriac slapped the table hard. 'Hector, I'm saying this to you now. I will not have this story told here.'

But Hector addressed himself to Bernard. 'It wasn't the Gestapo who raped her. They used—'

Mme. Auriac was on her feet. 'You will leave my table now, and never eat or drink here again!'

Hector hesitated, then he shrugged, and he was halfway out of his chair when June asked, 'They used what? What are you talking about, monsieur?'

The *Maire*, who had been so anxious to deliver his story, dithered over this direct question. 'It's necessary to understand, madame. . . . The Sauvy brothers saw this with their own eyes, through the window . . . and we heard later that this also used to happen at the interrogation centers in Lyon and Paris. The simple truth is, an animal can be trained—'

At last Mme. Auriac exploded. 'The simple truth? Since I'm the only one here, the only one in this village who knew Danielle, I'll tell you the simple truth!'

She stood erect, quivering with indignant fury. It was impossible, Bernard remembered thinking, not to believe her. The *Maire* was still in a half-standing position, which gave him a cringing appearance.

'The simple truth is that the Sauvy brothers are a couple of drunks, and that you and your cronies despised Danielle Bertrand because she was pretty and she lived alone and she didn't think she owed you or anyone else an explanation. And when this terrible thing happened to her, did you help her against the Gestapo? No, you took their side. You added to her shame with this story, this evil story. All of you, so willing to believe a couple of drunks. It gave you so much pleasure. More humiliation for Danielle. You couldn't stop talking about it. You drove that poor woman out of the village. But she was worth more than the lot of you, and the shame is on you, all of you, but especially you, Hector, with your position. And this is why I am telling you now, I never want to hear this disgusting story spoken of again. Do you understand? Never again!'

Mme. Auriac sat down. By not contesting her account, the *Maire* seemed to feel that he had earned the right to do the same. There was a silence while Monique cleared away the dishes.

Then June cleared her throat. 'And the dogs I saw this morning?'

The *Maire* spoke quietly. 'The same, madame. The Gestapo dogs. You see, it wasn't long afterward that everything changed. The Allies were landing in Normandy. When they started to break through, the Germans began pulling units up north to fight. This group here was doing nothing useful beyond intimidating the locals, so they were among the first to go. The dogs were left behind, and they ran wild. We didn't think they'd last, but they've lived off the sheep. For two years now they've been a menace. But don't you worry, madame. This afternoon, those two will be shot.'

And with his self-respect restored by his chivalrous promise, the *Maire* drained his glass again, filled it, and raised it. 'To the peace!'

But quick glances in Mme. Auriac's direction showed her sitting with folded arms, and the response to the *Maire*'s toast was only halfhearted.

After the cognac, the wine, and the protracted lunch, the *Maire* did not manage to dispatch a posse of villagers into the gorge that afternoon. Nor had anything happened by the following morning. Bernard was fretful. He was still set on the walk that had been spread before them at the Dolmen de la Prunarède. He wanted to go around to the *Maire*'s house immediately after breakfast. June, however, was relieved. She had matters to consider, and a strenuous walk no longer suited her. The homeward tug she had felt before was stronger than ever. Now she had a perfect rationalization for it. She made it clear to Bernard that even if she saw the dogs dead at her feet, she had no intention of walking down to Navacelles. He blustered, but she knew he understood. And Mme. Auriac, who served them herself at breakfast, understood too. She told them of a path *'doux et beau'* that ran in a southerly direction toward La Vacquerie, then ascended a hill before dropping down off the Causse into the village of Les Salces. Hardly a kilometer farther on was St. Privat, where she had cousins who would make them comfortable that night for the smallest consideration. Then they would have a pleasant day's walk into Lodève. Simple! She drew a map, wrote out the names and address of her cousins, filled the water bottles, gave them a peach each, and came a little way along the road before the exchange of little kisses to the cheek—then an exotic ritual for the English—and a special embrace for June.

The Causse de Larzac between St. Maurice and La Vacquerie is indeed gentler than the scrub wilderness farther west. I have walked it many times myself. Perhaps it is because the farmsteads, the *mas,* are closer together, and their benign influence on the landscape extends the whole way. Perhaps it is the ancient influence of the *polje,* a prehistoric riverbed that runs at right angles to the gorge. A half-mile stretch of lane, almost a tunnel, of wild rosebushes passes a dew pond in a field, which in those days was set aside by an eccentric old lady for donkeys too old to work. It was near here that the young couple lay down in a shady corner and quietly—for who knows who might have come along the lane—reestablished the sweet and easy union of two nights before.

They ambled into the village in the late morning. La Vacquerie used to lie on the main coach route from the Causse to Montpellier, before the road was built from Lodève in 1865. Like St. Maurice, it still has its hotel restaurant, and here Bernard and June sat on chairs on the narrow pavement with their backs to the wall, sipping beers and ordering lunch. June was silent again. She wanted to talk about the colored light she had seen or sensed, but she was certain that

Bernard would be dismissive. She also wanted to discuss the *Maire*'s story, but Bernard had already made it clear that he did not believe a word of it. A verbal contest was not what she wanted, but silence was inducing a resentment that would grow in the succeeding weeks.

Nearby, where the main road forked, stood an iron cross on a stone base. As the English couple watched, a mason cut in half a dozen fresh names. On the far side of the street, in the deep shadow of a doorway, a youngish woman in black was also watching. She was so pale that they assumed at first she had some sort of wasting disease. She remained perfectly still, with one hand holding an edge of her headscarf so that it obscured her mouth. The mason seemed embarrassed and kept his back to her while he worked. After a quarter of an hour, an old man in blue workman's clothes came shuffling along in carpet slippers and took her hand without a word and led her away. When the *propriétaire* came out, he nodded at the other side of the street, at the empty space, and murmured, *'Trois. Mari et deux frères'* as he set down their salads.

This somber incident remained with them as they struggled up the hill in the heat, heavy with lunch, toward the Bergerie de Tédenat. They stopped halfway up in the shade of a stand of pines before a long stretch of open ground. Bernard was to remember this moment for the rest of his life. As they drank from their water bottles, he was struck by the recently concluded war not as a historical, geopolitical fact but as a multiplicity, a near infinity of private sorrows, as a boundless grief minutely subdivided without diminishment among individuals who covered the continent like dust, like spores whose separate identities would remain unknown, and whose totality showed more sadness than any one could ever begin to comprehend; a weight borne in silence by hundreds of thousands, millions, like the woman in black for a husband and two brothers, each grief a particular, intricate, keening love story that might have been otherwise. It seemed as though he had never thought about the war before, not about its cost. He had been so busy with the details of his work, of doing it well, and his widest view had been of war aims, of winning, of statistical deaths, statistical destruction, and of postwar reconstruction. For the first time he sensed the scale of the catastrophe in terms of feeling—all those unique and solitary deaths, all that consequent sorrow, unique and solitary too, which had no place in conferences, headlines, history, and which had quietly retired to houses, kitchens, unshared beds, and anguished memories. This came upon Bernard by a pine tree in the Languedoc in 1946 not as an observation he could share with June but as a deep apprehension, a recognition of a truth that dismayed him into silence and, later, a question: what possible good could come of a Europe covered in this dust, these spores, when forgetting would be inhuman and dangerous, and remembering a constant torture?

June knew Bernard's description of this moment, but claimed to have no memory of the woman in black that was actually her own. When I walked through La Vacquerie in 1989 on my way to the dolmen, I found that the base of the monument was inscribed with Latin quotations. There were no names of the war dead.

By the time they reached the top, the mood had lightened again. They had a fine view back toward the gorge eight miles away, and they could trace their morning's walk as though on a map. It was here that they began to get lost.

Mme. Auriac's sketch did not make it clear how soon they had to leave the track that runs past the Bergerie de Tédenat. They turned off too soon, drawn down one of the enticing paths made by hunters that interlace across a heath of thyme and lavender. June and Bernard were not troubled. Scattered over the landscape were outcrops of dolomitic rock carved by the weather into towers and broken arches, and the impression was of walking through the ruins of an ancient village overrun by a delightful garden. They wandered happily in what they thought was the right direction for more than an hour. They were supposed to be looking for a wide sandy track, off which they would find the path that made the steep descent under the Pas de l'Azé and down into Les Salces. Even with the best of maps it would have been hard to find.

As the afternoon became early evening, they began to feel tired and exasperated. The Bergerie de Tédenat is a long, low barn that sits on the skyline, and they were trudging up the gentle incline that would take them back to it when they heard from the west a strange chock-chocking sound. As it approached them it broke up into a thousand points of melodious sound, as if glockenspiels, xylophones, and marimbas were competing in wild counterpoint. To Bernard it brought an image of cold water trickling over smooth rocks.

They stopped on the path and waited, enchanted. The first they saw was a cloud of ocher dust backlit by the low, still fierce sun, and then the first few sheep came around a bend in the path, startled by the sudden encounter but unable to turn back against the river of sheep surging behind them. Bernard and June climbed onto a rock and stood in the rising dust and clamor of bells, waiting for the flock to pass.

The sheepdog that trotted behind was aware of them as

it passed but paid them no attention. More than fifty yards back was the shepherd, the *berger*. Like his dog, he saw them and was entirely without curiosity. He would have passed with no more than a nod if June had not jumped onto the path in front of him and asked the way to Les Salces. It took him several paces to come to a complete stop, and he did not speak immediately. He wore the thick drooping mustache that was the tradition with *bergers* and the same wide-brimmed hat as theirs. Bernard felt like a fraud and wanted to take his own off. Thinking that her Dijonnais French might have been unintelligible, June was beginning to repeat herself slowly. The *berger* settled the frayed blanket he wore over his shoulders, nodded in the direction of his sheep, and walked on quickly to the head of the flock. He had muttered something they did not catch, but they assumed he wanted them to follow.

After twenty minutes the *berger* turned through a gap in the pines and the dog steered the flock through. Bernard and June had passed this way three or four times before. They found themselves standing in a small clearing on the edge of a cliff, with the lowering sun, the receding ridges of purplish low hills, and the distant sea spread before them. It was the very prospect they had admired in morning light from above Lodève three days before. They were on the edge of the plateau, about to descend. They were returning home.

Thrilled, already seized by an excited premonition of a joy that would fill her life, then Jenny's, then mine and our children's, June turned with sheep bumping her in the narrow space in front of the cliff edge to thank the *berger*. The dog was already edging the flock down a narrow cobbled path that ran under a great mass of rock, the Pas de l'Azé.

'It's so beautiful,' June shouted against the bells. The man looked at her. Her terms meant nothing to him. He turned, and they followed him down.

Perhaps thoughts of home were having their effect on the *berger* too, or perhaps (and this was Bernard's more cynical interpretation) he already had a plan in mind by becoming more talkative during the walk down. It was not usual, the *berger* explained, to bring the sheep off the Causse as early as this. The *transhumance* started in September. But his brother had died in a motorbike accident not so long ago and he was coming down to arrange various affairs. Two flocks would merge and some of the sheep would be sold off; there was property to sell and debts to settle. This account, with long pauses, took them along a path that descended through an oak wood, past a ruined *bergerie* which belonged to the man's uncle, across a dry gully, then through more holm oaks until they emerged finally around a hill topped with pines onto a broad sunlit shelf of terraced land which overhung a valley of vineyards and oaks. Down there, barely a mile away, was the village of St. Privat, perched on the edge of a small gorge cut by a tiny stream. Sitting comfortably among the hanging terraces, facing full down the valley into the setting sun, was a *bergerie* of gray stone. Immediately to one side was a small field, into which the dog was chasing the last of the sheep. Over to the north, rising sheer and bending around toward the northwest in a vast amphitheater of rock, were the cliffs of the plateau's edge.

The *berger* invited them to come and sit outside the *bergerie* while he went off to his spring for water. June and Bernard sat on a stone ledge with their backs to the warm irregular wall and watched the sun sink down behind the hills toward Lodève. As it did the light turned purplish, and through it a new cool breeze sifted, and the cicadas modulated their key. Neither spoke. The *berger* returned with a wine bottle full of water, and they passed it around. Bernard carved Mme. Auriac's peaches into pieces and shared them out. The *berger*, whose name they still did not know, had used up his conversation and retreated into himself. But his silence was soothing, companionable, and as they sat there, three in a row, June in the middle, watching the western sky flare, she felt a peace and spaciousness spread in her. Her contentment had a depth and tranquility that made her think she had never really known happiness before. What she had experienced two nights before at the Dolmen de la Prunarède had been a premonition of this, frustrated by busy talk, good intentions, schemes for improvements in the material conditions of strangers. What lay between that time and this were the black dogs and the oval of light, which she could no longer see but whose existence underpinned her joy.

She was safe on this little piece of land that crouched under the high cliff of the plateau. She was delivered into herself, she was changed. This, now, here. Surely this was what existence strained to be, and so rarely had the chance: to savor itself fully in the present, this moment in all its simplicity—the smooth darkening summer air, the scent of thyme crushed underfoot, her hunger, her slaked thirst, the warm stone she could feel through her shirt, the aftertaste of peach, the stickiness on her hand, her tired legs, her sweaty, sunny, dusty fatigue, this obscure and lovely place, and these two men, one whom she knew and loved, the other whose silence she trusted and who was waiting, she was certain, for her to take the next, inevitable step.

When she asked if she might see inside the *bergerie*, he seemed to be on his feet before her question was complete, and walking to the front door at the north end. Bernard said he was too comfortable to move. June followed the *berger* into total darkness. He lit a lamp and held it high for her. She advanced one or two paces and stopped. There was a sweet smell of straw and dust. She was in a long, barnlike structure with a pitched roof, divided into two stories by an arched stone ceiling, which had collapsed in one corner. The floor was packed earth. June stood in silence for a minute, and the man waited patiently. When at last she turned and asked, *'Combien?'* he was immediately ready with his price.

It cost the equivalent of thirty-five pounds, and came with twenty acres of land. June had enough saved at home to go ahead, but it was not until the following afternoon that she summoned the courage to tell Bernard what she had done. To her surprise, he did not try to oppose her with a barrage of sensible arguments about their needing to buy a house in England first, or the immorality of owning two houses when so many people everywhere were homeless. Jenny was born the following year, and June did not return to the *bergerie* until the summer of 1948, when she set in hand a number of modest improvements. Various new buildings in the local style were added to accommodate the growing family. The spring was properly tapped in 1955. In 1958 the electricity supply was installed. Over the years June repaired the terraces, tapped a second, smaller spring to irrigate the peach and olive orchards she had planted, and made a charming and very English maze out of the box shrubs that grew on the hillside.

In 1951, after her third child was born, June decided to live in France. Most of the time she kept the children with her. Occasionally, they had long periods with their father in London. In 1957 they attended the local schools in St. Jean de la Blacquière. In 1960 Jenny went to the lycée in Lodève. Throughout their childhood, the Tremaine children were posted back and forth between England and France, shepherded by kindly ladies on trains or by brisk Universal Aunts, between parents who would not live together or separate definitively. For June, convinced of the existence of evil and of God, and certain that both were incompatible with communism, found that she could neither persuade Bernard nor let him go. And he in his turn loved her and was infuriated by her self-enclosed life devoid of social responsibility.

Bernard left the party and became a 'voice of reason' during the Suez crisis. His biography of Nasser brought him to attention, and it was shortly after this that he became the lively, acceptable radical on BBC discussion programs. He stood as the Labour candidate in a by-election in 1961 and failed honorably. In 1964 he tried again and succeeded. It was about this time that Jenny went off to university, and June, fearing that her daughter was too much under Bernard's influence, wrote during her first term one of those old-fashioned, advice-filled letters that parents sometimes write to their departing children. In it June wrote that she had no faith in the abstract principles according to which 'committed intellectuals think to engineer social change.' All she could believe in, she told Jenny, 'are short-term, practical, realizable goals. Everyone has to take responsibility for his own life and attempt to improve it, spiritually in the first instance, materially if need be. I don't give a damn about a person's politics. As far as I'm concerned, Hugh Wall [a political colleague of Bernard's], whom I met last year at a dinner in London and who talked the whole evening over everyone at the table, is no better than the tyrants he loves to denounce . . .'

June published three books in her lifetime. In the mid-fifties, *Mystical Grace: Selected Writings of Saint Teresa of Avila.* A decade later, *Wildflowers of Languedoc,* and two years after that, a short practical pamphlet, *Ten Meditations.* As the years passed, her occasional trips to London became less frequent. She remained at the *bergerie,* studying, meditating, tending the property, until her illness forced her to England in 1982.

Recently I came across two pages of shorthand dating from my very last conversation with June, a month before she died in the summer of 1987: 'Jeremy, that morning I came face to face with evil. I didn't quite know it at the time, but I sensed it in my fear—these animals were the creations of debased imaginations, of perverted spirits no amount of social theory could account for. The evil I'm talking about lives in us all. It takes hold in an individual, in private lives, within a family, and then it's children who suffer most. And then, when the conditions are right, in different countries, at different times, a terrible cruelty, a viciousness against life erupts, and everyone is surprised by the depth of hatred within himself. Then it sinks back and waits. It's something in our hearts.

'I can see you think I'm a crank. It doesn't matter. This is what I know. Human nature, the human heart, the spirit, the soul, consciousness itself—call it what you like—in the end, it's all we've got to work with. It has to develop and expand, or the sum of our misery will never diminish. My own small discovery has been that this change is possible, it is within our power. Without a revolution of the inner life, however slow, all our big designs are worthless. The work we have to do is with ourselves if we're ever going to be at peace with each other. I'm not saying it'll happen. There's a good chance it won't. I'm saying it's our only chance. If it does, and it could take generations, the good that flows from it will shape our societies in an unprogrammed, unforeseen way, under the control of no single group of people or set of ideas . . .'

As soon as I had finished reading, Bernard's ghost was before me. He crossed his long legs and made a steeple of his fingers. ' "Face to face with evil"? I'll tell you what she was up against that day—a good lunch and a spot of malicious village gossip! As for the inner life, my dear boy, try having one of those on an empty stomach. Or without clean water. Or when you're sharing a room with seven others. Now of course, when we *all* have second homes in France. . . . You see, the way things are going on this overcrowded little planet, we *do* need a set of ideas, and bloody good ones too!'

June drew breath. They were squaring up.

Since June's death, when we inherited the *bergerie,* Jenny and I and our children have spent all our holidays here. There have been times in the summer when I have found myself alone in the last purple light of the evening, in the hammock under the tamarisk tree where June used to lie, wondering at all the world historical and personal forces, the huge and tiny currents, that had to align and combine to bring this place into our possession: a world war, a young couple at the end of it impatient to test their freedom, a government official in his car, the Resistance movement, the Abwehr, a penknife, Mme. Auriac's walk, *'doux et beau,'* a young man's death on a motorcycle, the debts his shepherd brother had to clear, and June's finding security and transformation on this sunny shelf of land.

But it is the black dogs I return to most often. They trouble me when I consider what happiness I owe them, especially when I allow myself to think of them not as animals but as spirit hounds, incarnations. June told me that throughout her life she sometimes used to see them, really see them, on the retina in the giddy seconds before sleep. They are running down the path into the gorge of the Vis, the bigger one trailing blood on the white stones. They are crossing the shadow line and going deeper, where the sun never reaches, and the amiable drunken mayor will not be sending his men in pursuit, for the dogs are crossing the river in the dead of night and forcing a way up the other side to cross the Causse; and as sleep rolls in they are receding from her, black stains in the gray of the dawn, fading as they move into the foothills of the mountains from where they will return to haunt us, somewhere in Europe, in another time.

The places mentioned in this novel correspond to actual French villages, but the characters associated with them are entirely fictional and bear no resemblance to persons living or dead. The *Maire's* story and the *Maire* himself have no basis in historical fact.

I.M.

ABOUT THE AUTHOR

Ian McEwan was born in 1948 and began writing in 1970. His first book, *First Love, Last Rites,* a collection of short stories, won the Somerset Maugham Award in 1976. His second collection of short stories, *In Between the Sheets,* was published in 1979. Among his other works are four novels—*The Cement Garden* (1978), *The Comfort of Strangers* (1981), *The Child in Time* (1987), and *The Innocent* (1990)—and a book of television dramas, *The Imitation Game & Other Plays* (1982).

Mr. McEwan lives in Oxford, England, with his wife and their four children.